Bad For My Thug

A Novel By
MISS JENESEQUA

Remember….
You haven't read 'til you've read #Royalty
Check us out at www.royaltypublishinghouse.com
#royaltydropsdopebooks

Text ROYALTY to 42828 for sneak peeks and
notifications when they come out!

Looking for a publishing home?

Royalty Publishing House, Where the Royals reside, is accepting submissions for writers in the urban fiction genre. If you're interested, submit the first 3-4 chapters with your synopsis to submissions@royaltypublishinghouse.com. Check out our website for more information: www.royaltypublishinghouse.com.

Be sure to <u>LIKE</u> our Royalty Publishing House
page on Facebook

For Josephine

I don't think you understand how amazing you are and all you do. Keep grinding. Keep hustling. You deserve all the success you've worked so hard for.

For Mama

You've been so supportive, understand and helpful. Surprised as you were… You still recognised that I had a true talent and allowed me to keep pursuing it. I love you so much and always will. Thank You God, for guiding me and strengthening me always.

- Jouir de! -

Miss Jenesegua

BY MISS JENESEQUA

ଓ *Lustful Desires: Secrets, Sex & Lies*

ଓ *Sex Ain't Better Than Love #1*

ଓ *Sex Ain't Better Than Love #2*

ଓ *Luvin' Your Man: Tales Of A Side Chick*

ଓ *Down For My Baller #1*

ଓ *Down For My Baller #2*

ଓ *Bad For My Thug*

"I'm a good girl... But I wanna be bad for you."
– Nicki Minaj

PROLOGUE

3.47pm.

Anika took another peek at the sexy specimen of a man sitting across from her and then dropped her eyes to the paperwork on her desk, willing herself not to look again. But it was hard as hell. He was sitting right across from her, waiting for his girlfriend to return to his side. Although he wasn't doing anything but staring at the screen of his cell phone, it was something about his aura that pulled her in...and not just her, other women in the waiting room had been stealing glances as well before they went on their merry way out.

Shifting in her seat, Anika looked up one more time and allowed her eyes to linger on the man sitting across from her desk, for what she was telling herself, was the last time. He was still staring at his cell phone, so she took the opportunity to let her eyes slowly inspect every inch of him. He had clear, caramel skin and a chiseled jawline, with light facial hair that formed a perfectly lined-up goatee. His hair was cut low, but he had soft waves that swirled around and gave him a pretty boy look. But it was obvious that he wasn't a pretty boy. He was dressed in sweatpants and a simple white tee with all white J's on his feet. And he was wearing two large gold chains, a flashy gold Rolex, and a diamond stud on each ear; this swagged out man had money... No doubt about it.

Damn, Anika thought to herself as she went back to his plump lips and focused in. Then, while she was looking, he flicked his pink tongue out of his mouth and licked his lips slowly. Call it attraction or sexual frustration from the fact that she hadn't had any in a while, Anika nearly creamed at the sight. She tore her attention away from his lips and then looked right into his grey eyes. He winked and she panicked. He was staring right at her.

Oh shit! Anika thought to herself as she lowered her eyes back to the papers on her desk and covered her face with her hands. She could feel her cheeks grow hot with embarrassment. He had caught her right in the act of eye-raping his body.

"So yo' pretty ass don't speak?"

His question caught her by surprise. He knew it too, because once she turned to stare at him, he could see the surprise in her pretty brown eyes.

Fuck, she is gorgeous! Blaze thought to himself.

Yeah, he was engaged but that didn't mean he couldn't look. Shit, he wasn't blind. As long as he didn't touch, Blaze knew Masika wouldn't be gunning for his ass.

As Blaze watched her struggle for a response, he had to chuckle to himself. This wouldn't be the first time that his aggressive nature had caught a woman off guard, but it was the first time that it had happened to a woman so beautiful. She was acting all embarrassed and shit like a nigga had never spoke game to her before. It was such a sharp contrast from Masika who was a hood chick and used to niggas trying to talk shit to her. She always had a good comeback waiting for anything someone tried to say, not like this chick. He took a minute to admire her look. She had long, wavy dark brown hair and the way it cascaded around her, made her seem like a goddess that he needed to please. Those red lips that he wanted to kiss and feel on every part of his body. That cute button nose of hers that he wanted to rub his own against and that perfect light skin of hers that made him want to massage lotion over her day and night.

Man, you gotta stop this shit. You engaged now, he tried to tell himself. But one more look at her and he ignored his own warning.

"I do speak," she responded shyly, surprised at how deep his baritone sounded. It was a voice so smooth, so sexy that it made her heat up with excitement and feel a small pool in her panties. "I'm just waiting for your fiancée to come back so I can escort you both to Attorney Coleman's office."

"Well, she probably takin' a shit," he commented amusingly, grinning widely and showcasing his pearly whites.

Anika kept silent at his crude words, rolling her eyes, and focused her attention back on her computer screen. The atmosphere became slightly awkward and tense, until Blaze decided that he wanted to break the ice with this pretty lady. "I'm Blaze," he introduced himself friendly.

Blaze... What an interesting name for an interesting man. Anika couldn't help but ponder in her private thoughts. *Obviously a nickname.*

"Anika," she said quickly, not bothering to look back at him. She didn't want to fall into the trap of letting those grey eyes win her over again.

"That's a real pretty name, ma'," he complimented her sweetly.

She felt her cheeks becoming hotter and even as she tried to stop herself blushing, she couldn't help it. Being light skinned definitely didn't help hide her blushing away from him.

"Thank you."

"No proble-"

Just before Blaze could finish his sentence, in came walking Masika, very annoyed. She stood right in front of Anika, blocking her view of Blaze completely and threw her hands on her hips.

"Why didn't you tell me the restrooms were bein' cleaned? I had to wait twenty minutes for that rude ass lady to finish cleaning, then to make matters worse she ain't even clean the damn place very well!"

The cleaning woman, Simona, always did an excellent job. That's why Anika convinced Attorney Coleman to hire her in the first place. Masika must have been tripping just because she had to wait.

"I apologize, Ms. Brooks. Please let me escort you and your fiancé to Attorney Coleman's office," Anika instructed her gently, as she stood up and smoothed down her black pencil skirt.

Masika rolled her eyes and sighed softly before reaching for Blaze's hand once he walked up beside her. Looking down briefly, Anika noticed that as soon as Masika reached for his hand, he didn't hold on to hers. He just let her hand linger on his and kept his grey eyes on Anika. Concealing a smirk, Anika turned around to lead them into the attorney's office. *Stop it Anika... He's engaged.*

But Anika couldn't help the way she suddenly felt about this fine nigga. Call it whatever you liked, but Anika was definitely feeling Blaze and she had a feeling that he was feeling her too.

However, once opening Attorney Coleman's door for Blaze and his fiancé, Anika couldn't help but feel a small hint of jealousy at the way Blaze had his arm wrapped lovingly around her curvy waist, as they walked in to meet their new attorney.

You see Anika? He's completely taken.

CHAPTER 1~ OLD MEMORIES

~ 2 Months Prior ~

Anika sighed deeply as she stared down at his text message.

"Wifey's got something planned tonight baby. Sorry. I'll make it up 2 u x"

She hated this.

His wifey meant nothing to him so why was he still with her? Anika didn't understand why he couldn't just leave his wife and be with her. She had been working with Jamal Coleman for almost a year now, and throughout their working together she had treated him well. She had treated him good in all the ways he wanted and more, even going that extra mile for him in the office when he had been having a bad day. Anika wasn't sure what exactly she felt for Jamal, but she knew that it was quickly growing stronger and stronger every single day.

This nigga had her going on cloud nine every single time they fucked each other's brains out. With his large anaconda and her pretty kitty, they made great teammates. He never failed to make her feel good and that's one of the many things she loved about him.

His wife wasn't important, but all Anika wished was that he ditched her and come fuck with a real bitch - her. The one that gave his dick that special TLC and never let him go unsatisfied.

Anika was just hoping that Jamal ditched her very soon because being a side piece wasn't going to be enough anymore.

***

"Blaze! Baby... Oooo! Baby, feels so gooooooood," Masika moaned passionately to him, wrapping her legs tighter around his torso. He continued to quickly pump in and out for her, feeling his body heat up with desire at how good and right her pussy felt around his dick. She was taking all of him like a pro and it only made Blaze happier at how she was loving his stroke.

"Feels good you say girl?"

"Mmm! Yesssssss Daddy, so good!" He just the loved the way her responses encouraged him to keep murdering her pussy and not to hold back on anything.

"You love this dick?"

"I love it," she answered sexily, clawing her long nails into his muscular back as she continued to meet him, stroke for stroke.

"Tell me how much you fuckin' love it," he whispered seductively into her ear, gently biting on it as he continued to ride her.

Blaze couldn't help but contemplate on the first day he met Masika, two years ago in her sister's apartment.

What a night he had just had. Desiree was really something. With the skills she had, Blaze was sure that she had to be a porn star or something. She was way too experienced, more experienced than any other girl he had been with this whole month. But hey, at least he finally got some.

Blaze didn't want to wake her up. He wanted to get his shit, put his clothes on and go. He had important work to attend to.

Gently, Blaze began to stir in the bed trying his hardest not to wake Desiree up. All he wanted was to get out of here, but the way her head was resting against his chest made it seem nearby impossible.

Just as Blaze began to shift again, attempting to move his body away from hers, Desiree was up. A soft yawn sounded out her mouth and Blaze watched her carefully through hooded eyes as she began to stretch.

Those long arms and legs hit Blaze's face and legs, causing him to groan, annoyed at her.

"Oh sorry baby," she apologized softly, opening her eyes fully.

Baby?

Oh hell nah. Blaze knew that if there was a better time to leave, it was now. Desiree was probably starting to catch feelings, something that Blaze couldn't allow. He couldn't have her thinking that he belonged to her. No, he belonged to no one but himself. Pussy was just pussy, which he needed at least four times a week.

"It's a'ight," he responded in a low voice, lifting himself off the red pillow behind his head.

Desiree removed her head from his chest, seeing that he was now sitting upright. She was hoping that he wasn't planning to leave so soon. Another couple rounds of that dick would do her some good this morning.

"I had fun last night Blaze," she announced happily, turning on her side to face him. Staring into those grey eyes would never get boring for her. He was just such a beautiful man.

With that handsome chocolate face, that 6'3" height, those grey eyes, those juicy pink lips, that muscular physique, those endless abs, those fresh layer of waves that sat on his head, Desiree didn't want to stop fucking Blaze. Even though this had been a one night thing so far, she wanted things to go further.

"I had fun last night too," he replied nonchalantly.

"And I wanna do this again," she stated with a grin, still gazing into those gorgeous eyes of his.

"You do?"

"Yes Blaze, I really do," she reiterated lifting one of her hands to rub on his hard chest. "You're sexy, ambitious and amazing in bed... I want to be your girl Blaze."

Blaze stared down at her in confusion. What the hell was she talking about? They had only met yesterday at Marquise's club, talked a little then went back to hers for meaningless sex. That was it.

Sex.

"Look... Diamond, I'm no-"

"My name's not Diamond, it's Desiree," she snapped, cutting him off instantly.

Blaze cursed himself in his head for bringing up the chick he had fucked two nights ago in his silver Mustang. And from the irritated look on Desiree's face, he could tell she wasn't happy with him that he had forgotten her name.

But oh fucking well.

"Look Desiree... I'ma be honest wit'chu... I ain't lookin' for a relationship right now."

"Why not?" she queried with a frown.

"I'm too busy for all that," he said. *"You know what I do... So being with someone right now ain't an option."*

"But let me be the one to change your mind Blaze. I could be your ride or die chick. Your trap queen."

Blaze couldn't help but smirk at her words. She was a funny one. However, Desiree wasn't playing and once she realized he wasn't really taking her seriously, she decided she needed to take matters into her own hands. She wasn't letting this fine nigga go. Not when he was rich, feared and respected by all!

Desiree quickly got up on her knees and straddled Blaze with her covers underneath her. The covers that were hiding his under nakedness and his hidden manhood away from her. That didn't mean she couldn't feel it.

"Blaze, I love you!" she cooed loudly, placing her hands on his shoulders and pulling him closer into her naked body.

What the hell? Blaze was suddenly confused. What was wrong with this crazy chick? As much as those titties stuck out, perky and ready for him to play with, Blaze needed to get out of here.

"What'chu mean? You don't even know me girl."

"I know enough! And I know that you and I will make some pretty ass kids together and build an empire together."

This bitch is crazy, Blaze mused to himself now staring at her with disgust.

"Desiree, what the hell you talkin' 'bout?"

"Like... I wanna be with you forever, Blaze," she stated in an affectionate tone. "I was just thinking about our kid's name... Our kid's name could be something mysterious and magical just like yours."

Huh? Blaze officially knew that he had fucked up messing with this chick.

"Damn you got some good ass hair Blaze, fuck," she suddenly commented, touching up on his fresh layer of waves. "With that hair we gon' have at least five or six kids."

"Desiree, what the fuck - girl no," he retorted. "You feeling alright? I ain't having no kids, certainly not five or six with'chu, that's a fuckin' lot."

"A lot before we get married," she added with a delighted smile. "You needa put a ring on my motherfucking finger baby before I push anything out this pussy for you."

Blaze couldn't help but continue to stare at her with confusion and disgust. She was clearly delusional.

"I'm thinking we should have a wedding at a tropical place, somewhere I can show my personality. I can wear like a bikini and you could wear a pink thong and there will be flamingos and elephants! And a whole bunch of just wild shit, you know what I mean?" She questioned him with a crazed look in her honey brown eyes.

"That's not gon' work ma'," Blaze replied.

"You don't think that's gon' work?" she asked rudely with an arched brow. "Of course that's not gon' work. I haven't gone through your phone yet," she announced with a shrug, before diverting her eyes to the lamp stand nearby. "Is this it right here?"

Blaze didn't respond and just looked at her rudely. He even quickly slapped her hand away when she tried to grab his phone off the stand.

"Shoot, I can clear my schedule, I got time today. We can go through all your side bitches, all your messages... I just need to see

who you're dealing with you know, so I can make sure that they don't pop back up. What's your password?"

Blaze sighed deeply, his frustrations building with the woman currently straddled on his hard on, which was slowly going limp with every word Desiree said.

"I need to go through all your messages; all your Facebook messages, your Instagram messages, your Twitter messages, I need to see everything. I need your passwords to everything because I will be damned if there's some side bitch trying to come and take my spot because I. Do. Not. Play. That. Shit. Nigga!" she shouted loudly in his face, pressing her hands deeper into his shoulder blades. "Okay?" she queried with a sudden fake smile.

Blaze didn't know what to say, all he needed was to get the hell out of here.

"Look Desiree, I gotta g-"

She instantly cut him off with a loud piercing scream, "Ahhh! I gotta call my mom and tell her I found my man! Oh my gosh, she gon' tell everyone at church and we gon' throw a big party... Do you like brunch? Do you like lobster?"

"Umm... N-"

"You know what though, I'm allergic to lobster and I need you to know that because if I die... It's gon' be on you. And I'ma get you. My whole family gon' get you."

Blaze didn't bother listening to anything this crazy lady had to say. She was talking absolute bullshit and Blaze had no time to spare listening to the rest of her crap today.

He pushed her off him, resulting in Desiree to land on her original bed position. He frantically rushed out her bed eager to get out her apartment.

"Blaze, where you going?!"

"Away from yo' crazy ass," he snapped, quickly putting his black Ralph Lauren boxers on and picking up his clothes that lay scattered on the carpeted floor.

"No, stay!" she protested, reaching out to grab onto him.

"Nah, I'm out," Blaze concluded before grabbing his smartphone and rushing out her bedroom.

He was never messing around with her again, that was for sure. His bomb ass dick had made her turn into one crazy bitch.

"Blaze!"

He ignored her calls for him and continued running towards her exit. When finally swinging her oak door open, there she was staring at him carefully before sighing softly and rolling her eyes at his half-naked state.

Those honey brown eyes, that pretty face, long ponytail and banging body underneath all those tight clothes, instantly had Blaze infatuated with her. Here stood a beauty that he knew he had to have. Even if it was for just one night.

Now here she lay, two years later and in his arms.

"I love you Blaze," Masika said lovingly with a sigh.

"I love you too baby."

Moments like these came rare, especially with Blaze's busy schedule running the streets and making money. So any opportunity Masika had for cuddling with her man, she took it. Pressing her body closer against his, Masika found herself grinning extra hard and Blaze quickly noticed.

"Why you grinnin' extra hard Mas?" he questioned her curiously, with a smirk that was now growing on his lips.

"Because I'm happy," she responded gently. "Being your future wifey and all."

Proposing to Masika last month wasn't something Blaze had really planned. Sure they had had their ups and downs these past years, a few breakups, a few side chicks and a few lies. But the love they shared was real and Blaze figured he might as well settle down with the woman who he had been with for so long.

"That's real good to hear beautiful," he gently cooed in her ear, stroking her soft cheek.

"And as your future wifey I want something."

"What's that Mas?"

"I want to have your baby, Blaze."

Blaze immediately began to pout. This is the shit that she loved to bring up on a regular, but he didn't love.

"We talked 'bout this Masika," he stated in a low tone as he began shifting his body away from hers. "When you finally divorce that fool, you can have all my babies," he reminded her.

"But baby, I want us to start now."

"No Masika," he snapped at her in a dismissive tone. "You and I can't do shit 'til you divorce him. I don't really get why you ain't tryin' to leave him. Do you not want to be with me? You still want that nigga?"

"No Blaze, I want you. I want us to be married. I want our own family."

"Well you kno' what you need to do," Blaze declared. "Divorce him, then we'll get married and you can have my babies. A'ight?"

She nodded quickly before leaning her body back into Blaze's, holding onto his strong, muscular arms.

Masika knew what she needed to do. She couldn't lose her man because of her laziness of not getting things done in time. And there was absolutely no way that she was letting him go so he could easily fall back into his lifestyle of fucking bitches left, right and center.

Divorcing Leek needed to be done sooner not later, because Masika wanted to marry her man now. She wanted to be the mother of all his children. No one else but her had that rightful title. It belonged to her alone.

All she needed was a divorce attorney and a way to figure out how she was getting Tarique to understand that she wasn't going to ever get back with his father. She also needed to figure out a way to finally tell Blaze that she had a child with her soon to be ex-husband, Leek. Because keeping this secret away from him just wasn't going to work anymore.

CHAPTER 2 ~ LOYALTY FIRST

"Blaze… Please… I would never betray you or the Knight Nation… Don't do this man, please! Kareem tell him, ple-"

"Shut yo' ass up fool!" Kareem shouted angrily, suddenly hitting Haneef with the butt of his black pistol, resulting in Haneef to fall back in pain.

"I'm going to talk to Leek today and tell him that I'm making moves to finalize our divorce. See you later baby? I'm cooking your favorite tonight… With that matching lingerie you love so much." Blaze couldn't help but smile at the recent text message from Masika. She always knew the right words to say.

He quickly locked his black iPhone and placed it in his back pocket, before diverting his attention to the man on his knees in front of him. His lip was bleeding and both of his eyes were now bruised and beaten up. Kareem had decided to let out some steam once Haneef had been brought in.

Being the head of the Knight Nation had it's rough days for Blaze. Today was definitely one of those rough days. When Blaze was forced to make a decision about one of his squad members, he had no choice but to follow through.

Haneef was on his knees surrounded in the middle, as Blaze, Kareem and Marquise stared down upon him intensely. The guilty look on Haneef's face told Blaze everything he needed to know. Haneef had stepped out against the Knight Nation and thought he would get away with it. But no.

Blaze had eyes everywhere. With his many trap houses, crack houses and workers under his nation, Blaze was a god in his own right. Also, Kareem and Marquise were his two right hand men that he could count on for everything, including holding the business down when Blaze was busy with his other more legal businesses. Ever since the three of them dropped out of high school thirteen years ago, and decided that the education system wasn't for them, they knew they were sticking together forever.

"Man Blaze, end this fool already," Kareem insisted as his eyes glared into Haneef's scared brown pools. "He don't deserve to live no more for what's he done."

"I agree," Marquise stated with a smirk. "This nigga done messed up our profits. He thought he was going to get away with cheatin' us but he's been clocked. Silly motherfucker. You already know how I feel about this bitch ass fool. Just dead him B'."

Blaze listened carefully to each of his boys' words, understanding their feelings for wanting Haneef dead at this exact moment in time. Shit, he wanted him dead too. Haneef had been stealing and cheating away from the Knight Nation for months. While he went out to sell some product, he purposely stashed some away, kept profits and constantly lied against fellow colleagues.

Blaze hadn't noticed it at first, until a loyal worker at one of his trap houses in downtown Atlanta knew the girl who had been fucking around with Haneef, and snitched to him. He straight away told Marquise since Blaze wasn't always around, and that's how this situation was brought to his attention.

It was rare to see people trying to fuck with Blaze. Not many tried it because they knew that he wasn't one to fuck with. He was a ruthless, cold blooded murderer. He didn't talk much, didn't waste time – he just got shit done.

"So what'chu wan' do Blaze? I'm thinking we cut him open and let the suckers on him," Kareem voiced in a tone that had a high hint of excitement.

The suckers sounded like a good idea to Blaze because those motherfucking dogs were always so damn hungry. They were Rottweilers and didn't waste any time when it came to making sure that a human deserved what they got. The only thing that Blaze hated about the suckers was that they created way too much mess.

"Too messy Reem," Blaze said shaking his head in disapproval, as he began to walk around Haneef further intimidating him. "I say we… do somethin' more painful."

"Hmm… What you thinkin'?" Marquise queried curiously, gently stroking his freshly shaved chin.

Blaze continued to contemplate to himself for a while, thinking about what was the best punishment for Haneef's betrayal. He didn't just want to kill him as that would just make things too easy and it would make things seem like Blaze let people off easily for fucking with him when he didn't. He made people suffer because that's what they deserved.

"I'm thinkin' we teach Haneef a real lesson today about crawlin' in secret holes and being a snake," Blaze revealed with a twinkle in his grey eyes. "Let's get the drills out boys."

Ten minutes later, Blaze, Marquise and Kareem had their own individual drills in their hands and ready to go. They were suited up in white bodysuits so they wouldn't stain their expensive clothes and had goggles protecting their eyes from any splats. Haneef was currently naked and tied up so that he couldn't move while they began their work on him. Kareem had also duct taped his mouth so that his screams would be kept to a minimum.

It didn't really matter whether or not his screams could be heard because they were in one of Blaze's warehouses that, to the public eye, looked abandoned.

"Don't fight it nigga… Just enjoy it," Marquise cooed gently in Haneef's ear before switching his drill on.

Blaze just wanted him to make sure that before he died, Haneef would remember the biggest mistake of his life by betraying the Knight Nation.

Loyalty first, or lose your life.

***

"Fuck, Leek...Agh!" she loudly moaned. This wasn't something that she had planned to happen. It just happened... more than five times a month.

The hard smacking noise of their bodies colliding together, echoed in the bathroom. Leek tightened his hold on her hips, rocking her body hard, up and down on his dick, which was only getting harder and harder by the second.

He groaned deep with each thrust, massaging his hands against her warm skin and she couldn't help but continue to moan as the thrusts kept coming through. He leaned down, still pumping his hips, pressing close to her ear. "What I tell you 'bout givin' my pussy away girl?" Leek kissed behind her ear, leaning back up to continue his assault on her tight pussy.

"Leek... Oh shit!" If dicks could kill Masika knew she would be one dead woman right now. Leek wasn't showing her any mercy and she knew exactly why. Leek was her baby daddy and soon to be ex-husband, but Blaze was the love of her life... right?

It's not her fault that Leek's dick was like magic and kept her falling back into his trap over and over again. Yeah she fucked the baby daddy from time to time, but that didn't mean shit. Blaze was the one she was going to be with forever. He had proposed and all she needed to do so they could start planning their wedding, was to divorce Leek.

With every pull of his dick, Masika found herself unable to control the way her mouth sounded and the way she was feeling because of Leek's amazing stroke. He moved his hand over her ass, squeezing her soft flesh before delivering a quick spank.

"Oooh baby," she moaned deeply, arching her back. She loved it when he got dominating with her and made her feel like a bad girl that needed to be punished.

He pulled back his hand again, smacking her cheeks with another hard blow. "Tell me what I wan' hear baby," he panted hard, massaging her hot skin. She knew exactly what he wanted to hear but the words weren't for him. They were for her fiancé only.

Leek kept one hand latched to her hip while the other started teasing her stiff nipples. He rolled and squeezed them between his thick fingers. He pinched them hard, thrusting his shaft deeper inside her.

"Leek... Uhh…" He was killing her pussy, murdering it in fact, as he continued to pound in and out of her. Masika always noticed how much Leek loved hitting it from the back. It was his favorite position because he constantly loved spanking her.

He slowly slid his hand from her hip, dipping his fingers between her legs and pressing down hard on her swollen clit. His fingers rubbed quickly over her slippery pussy, pumping his dick faster into her hot slit. "Tell me what I want to hear Masika."

"Leek... Oh my..." Her moans were uncontrollable, as his fingers began to work on her pussy making her want to scream out in pleasure. "Uhh...uhhhh... Uhhh," she whined, unable to form words as the pleasure intensified deep inside her. "F-f-fuuuuuck!" she cried, throwing her head back, her hair sweeping over her naked shoulders, sticking to her sweaty skin.

He looked up only to stare at her gorgeous reflection in the mirror in front of them. "Tell me Mas." Her eyes fluttered shut in pure ecstasy, and her whole body shook with pleasure. Her pussy clenched tightly then pulsed hard, releasing her hot juices all over his dick.

"Uhh... It's yours Leek, my pussy's yours." She shuddered to the feeling of her cum coating his entire dick. She was done for and it was all because of him. He had made her cum so the least she could do was make him feel appreciated by gassing him up a little.

Moving his hands back to her hips, he dug his hands into her skin, thrusting a few hard pumps before freezing behind her. "Fuck!" he groaned, shaking hard as his release filled her insides.

Ten minutes later, Masika was sitting on the edge of her pink California king sized bed waiting for Leek to get out her bathroom.

She needed to come clean to him today. He was already aware of the fact that she was with Blaze – everyone knew she was with Blaze. However, today was the day that she put an end to their little side fucks. She loved Blaze, wanted to marry him and move into that big mansion of his.

At the moment, their living arrangement was complicated. Yes, he had proposed but she wasn't living with him. He either spent time at her apartment or they met up somewhere, but she never stayed in his mansion in Buckhead. The only time she had been there was when he was sick one time and needed her to play nurse. But other than that, Masika was never at Blaze's mansion.

It bothered her very much, but she understood that Blaze was more of a traditional man. Even though he was a drug dealer and owned one of the largest drug cartels in the whole city of Atlanta, he still did things traditionally.

He wanted a stay-at-home wifey, popping his babies out left, right and center, cooking in his kitchen, and a wifey who he could trust with his entire empire just in case anything happened to him.

Masika knew she was that woman. She was his wifey. His trap queen. And there was absolutely no way that she was going to give her rightful position up. Sure she had only been with Blaze for about two years, but two years was enough for her to be his forever.

When Leek finally came out her bathroom, Masika couldn't help but stare at him with nothing but lust.

They were due to be divorced but goddamn it this man wasn't fine! Everything about him was fine. From those long dark brown dreadlocks, that handsome face, those green eyes, to that fair light skin, that sexy muscular physique… Leek was gorgeous and all Masika wanted to do was eat him up. But no!

Today she got straight down to the business and ended things between them. This divorce needed to be done because she needed to marry her man and finally get her own closet space in that large mansion of his.

"Leek, I need that divorce now," she blurted out quickly, as he walked up to her in nothing but a white towel. Those hard, chiseled abs looked so good wet, and her tongue was suddenly twitching and watering up because she wanted to lick them.

"Why?" He queried with a frown, still walking up to her bedside and once he reached her, he lifted her chin up so she could stare directly into his green eyes as he spoke. "You got a son with me, you don't need that nigga no more."

"But I love hi-"

He cut her off, "You love me."

"Leek, I'm engaged to him. You and I aren't the way we used to be, you know this. I need to be with Blaze," she explained with a pout, as he still held her chin up so she was forced to look up at him.

"So why you keep fuckin' me on a daily if you need to be with his dumb ass?" Leek asked incredulously.

"It's just a bit of fun," she mumbled quietly. "But no more Leek... Please, I need to be with him."

"You love him that much, but you cheat on him? That ain't love Mas," he told her simply before letting her chin go.

"I do love him," she stated, trying to reassure Leek that she did. All she wanted was this divorce and she would be free to marry her man. "I need this divorce Leek. We don't love each other anymore, we see other peop-"

"Who said I didn't love you Mas?" he questioned her with a frown, glaring down at her with those green eyes.

"You don't love me," she said with a sigh. "So please don't try some bullshit with me today Leek. Look, I'm finding a divorce attorney by the end of the week and when he or she comes to you with the papers, I need you to sign."

Leek said nothing and just continued to glare down at Masika, but from the pissed look in his eyes, Masika knew he wasn't happy with her words.

"We'll have joint custody of Tarique, you'll see him just like you're seeing him now and everything will be fine. I don't want much from you, only a check a month for Tarique and that's all."

Leek owned his own drug cartel too, but Masika didn't want anything from that. He earned peanuts in comparison to Blaze. All she wanted was for him to care for his son just like he was now and all would be good.

Masika observed Leek carefully as he kept silent, clearly pondering in his thoughts before finally responding, "A'ight. So how Blaze feel 'bout Tarique spendin' some nights with me and some nights with you?"

Masika couldn't answer his question and all she could do was look down in shame. She had no idea how Blaze felt about Tarique because Blaze didn't even know Tari existed. Just as Masika finally figured out the words to say to Leek, she felt her chin being thrust up and her eyes forced to look into Leek's green ones.

"You sneaky bitch," he laughingly commented, his green eyes lighting up like diamonds. "He still don't know?"

"I... I was gon' tell hi-"

"Oh, well you gon' need to tell him real soon Mas," he explained with a large, evil grin that seemed to be getting bigger and bigger by the second. "You want your divorce?" She nodded willingly with his hand still tightly cupped around her chin. "Then tell him 'bout Tarique."

Only the Lord knew how Masika was going to tell Blaze about her three-year-old, because she had no clue.

CHAPTER 3 ~ WANTING MORE

"Thank you Jamal... You're the best honestly. Because of you I'm now free from that jerk and richer than I was before."

This is what he did. This is what he was the best at. Winning his cases and making his clients very happy and making sure that their pockets got fatter so his could too... once they eventually paid him. And Anika was given a front row seat to his whole operation.

Anika knew how much Jamal loved being a divorce attorney because with being an attorney came commitment, dedication and perseverance. No one could deny it, he was amazing at what he did.

Being a divorce attorney's assistant meant that she was well paid, learning from one of the best and getting that D whenever she could. Whatever you desired, whether it was the puppy, the house, the car or the money – Jamal was here to make sure that you got it all.

Anika sighed softly as she settled deeper into her black office chair trying her hardest to relax. Jamal had just won his last case for one of her clients, and boy oh boy was it a challenge. A challenge because his client's husband's attorney was just as bad as as he was. But Anika didn't worry the slightest, she knew Jamal had everything under control.

Straight outta Compton, crazy motherfucker named Ice Cube.
From the gang called Niggaz With-

"Hey girl!" Once Ice Cube's loud, bold voice sounded through the office, Anika knew exactly who was calling her right now.

"Nika! You done with work for today?" Her best friend questioned her curiously, clearly trying to get her to come out somewhere with her today.

"Umm... I should be in a few minutes... Why?" Anika queried suspiciously, turning in her seat so she could look up at the white digital clock hanging on the nude wallpaper.

"You already know why baby... Meet me at our spot in two hours?"

"Umm... Yea-" Suddenly Anika's attention was diverted to the opening white door across from where she sat.

"Nika, you there?"

Looking straight ahead, Anika's excitement increased as he stepped in deeper to the room, with the champagne bottle in his hand and the two empty glasses.

This sexy man...

"Uh, yeah hun, two hours, yeah?" She questioned Sadie, biting her lips sexily as he walked towards her. She was trying to confirm the details for her lunch date quickly, so she could tend to this fine man. They had a lot of celebrating to do.

"Yeah, see you in a bit."

Once Sadie hung up, Anika smiled seductively at him, staring into his mesmerizing brown pools.

"Baby, I have something to say," he began sweetly, placing the two champagne glasses on the mahogany table in front of Anika.

"What is it?" she queried softly.

"Well, we definitely have to celebrate for the case we won today but... I can't take you out as planned."

"Why not?" she questioned rudely, no longer feeling as pleased as she was before. This nigga was not about to cancel on her. "You said we were going to celebrate together to-"

He gently cut her off, "And we are beautiful... Just not right now. Angelica has organized lunch with her parents and you know I can't miss that. They'll be on my case for ages."

Anika didn't give a fuck about Angelica or her stupid ass parents. She was Jamal's wife and for that, Anika would always despise her. She was always coming in between their quality time together. Like she didn't see the nigga every single, fucking night. She was so selfish to Anika, one of the many reasons why she hated her.

Anika reluctantly kept silent and stared off into the modern space around her. She found herself staring at the nude walls, black furniture and green plants calming and soothing because she felt like she was going to off on this nigga. Pissed off was an understatement for her feelings right now.

However, once Jamal made his way around the desk and bent low in-between her thighs, pulling her skirt down and pulling her pink thong to the side, pissed off quickly disappeared.

"I promise to make it up to you real soon sweetheart... Don't be angry with daddy."

***

"Wait, so he gave you bomb ass head but you're still angry with him? Damn girl, you really are a tough bitch," Sadie announced with a light chuckle before taking a sip of her champagne.

Meet Sadie Clark. Anika's Holy Grail, ride or die chick and sister from another mother. Ever since she had met Sadie back in high school, she knew that this was the only chick that she needed to be friends with for the rest of her life.

They didn't seem to have a single thing in common at first, but soon realized how much they both loved the hip-hop group N.W.A and loved the whole West Coast hip-hop movement in general. From their joint love of the same music came the same love of food, fashion and ambition. Not to forget they both lost their parents in fatal crashes. For Anika's parents, it was a plane crash and for Sadie's parents, it was a car crash.

Sadie was one beautiful lady. Her mother was of Nigerian descent and her father Dominican and because of this Sadie was born with the most flawless, milk chocolate skin, thick but long curly hair, and a banging body that came with long legs, curves and a large African ass that could be seen from the front. At 5'6" with that firm ass and gorgeous face, Sadie was living the good life as a nail technician/makeup artist.

Everyone who was anyone in Atlanta went to Sadie to get their nails and makeup done because she was the best at what she did. With her super kit and her amazing skills, Sadie beat all the pretty ladies' face with the best cosmetics in the world and made your nails look good enough to eat.

"He even rushed it, pissing me off further. Why should I be happy with him when he keeps choosing his dumb wife over me?" Anika queried curiously, as she stared down at her menu in her hands thinking about what she was going to order. Lord knew that she was hungry and happy that her best friend had decided to treat her out today.

"But I thought you guys were just fuck buddies, nothing more?" Sadie responded simply.

"Yeah, we were before... But I think now I'm falling for him and he's falling for me too."

"So you're trying to become wifey then?"

Anika looked up from her menu to stare into her best friend's brown pools. "I don't know... All I know is that I want more than being his little side piece all the time. You know what I mean?"

"I hear you babe," Sadie replied gently. "But are you sure you're down for all the drama that's gonna come your way with his wife, as you claim her spot?"

Anika stiffly shook her head no before saying, "You know I don't give a fuck about no bummy ass wife. She doesn't treat him right; I can tell by the way he's always trying his hardest to get some off me. Taking her spot will be a no brainer."

"Do you think he would want you as his wife though?"

"Why would he not? I fuck him good, I listen to him and I understand him. He never gets tired of me but always gets tired of her."

"And that pussy of yours certainly doesn't get tired of him either," Sadie commented with a large grin.

"Dick way, way too bomb. You know I don't like fucking with married men, but there's just something about him... We just connect. It's not just sex."

"Well if you say so girl, and you know no matter what I've always got your back and will be here for you."

***

9.43pm.

Lunch with Sadie had turned into drinks at a local night club with Sadie, and before Anika knew it drinks had turned into the strip club with Sadie.

Anika couldn't help how she felt about strip clubs, especially when Sadie was involved. Some would say that Sadie was a bad influence on Anika, but Anika would say that she was just her wild sister from another mother who knew how to have fun the right way.

So after dropping all those ones on the baddest stripper, Candi at Cheetah Longue, Anika was relieved to finally be tucked into her warm California bed and ready to catch some much needed rest. The only thing that was on her mind was Jamal. He hadn't texted or called her since work and she was starting to feel disappointed again at the fact that they weren't celebrating tonight. The only thing she could do now was rest and try to forget about it.

However, that rest wasn't coming anytime soon once Anika's doorbell suddenly rang, making her not only annoyed but confused at who was coming over to her apartment at this time.

Reluctantly, Anika got out of bed in nothing but her black lace bra and matching panties and went to answer her door. Her first guess was that Sadie had come to see her for some reason, so she didn't bother checking the peephole to see who was on the other side. But as soon as her door swung open, she instantly loved opening the door for him.

In front of her stood a sex god, towering over her at 6'1", with that smooth chocolate skin, that freshly low-cut fade, those mesmerizing brown eyes, those cute dimples and that sexy grin that used to bring her so much joy in the past.

"Jamal, what are yo-" She was cut off when he crashed his soft lips to hers. His hands went straight for her hips, making her moan gently as he kicked her door shut behind him. He flipped her around, pushing her back against the hard door. This was a game that she always played with him when he unexpectedly came to her apartment, like she didn't know why he was here and like she didn't want him.

She sighed as he broke the kiss, moving his smooth lips to kiss her hungrily along the curve of her neck. She tilted her head up, as his wet lips quickly kissed down the curve of her neck. "Jamal…" She bit down on her lip as she felt his hands move towards her hard breasts that were hidden underneath her black bra. She had definitely missed those big hands touching her everywhere. She knew he knew how bad she wanted him right now.

"Jamal, stop," she moaned softly to the heavenly feel of his big hands touching her breasts. All she wanted to do was get completely naked for him and take this to her bedroom. But no, she had to stay strong. She couldn't give into his seduction so easily.

"You don't want me to stop though baby," he whispered gently in her ear. "I know you want me right now." He gently planted a soft kiss on her ear. "And I want to show you just how sorry I am for not celebrating with you today at the office long enough and not taking you out."

She gasped as he pinched her hard nipples. "I plan to show you… Over and over and over again..." *My God,* Anika knew this man was trying to drive her insane. Her pussy was now purring for him. "…Until the only thing you'll be screaming tonight is my name."

Oh shit.

He then used his hands to pull both of her legs up around his hips. Her hands reached for his shoulders and he pushed her harder up against the wall.

Fuck pretending to fight him right now.

It didn't take long for them to strip the remaining clothes from each other's bodies. Even as they were still against the wall, Jamal continued to drive Anika insane. He lifted her high up on the wall, kissing every part of her now naked body.

Every kiss drove her insane to the point of no return. He took his time and effort, planting delicate kisses in every single place he could get his thick lips on. "Baby... Mmm..." Anika couldn't stop moaning and he hadn't even started fucking her yet, but she was still left very excited for his plans.

He kissed her again, their lips and their tongues smacking, snaking around each other's. Their mouths were drawn together like super-charged magnets; they didn't want to stop either. But once Jamal pulled away from her lips, she quickly tried to pull him back on to her lips.

"No baby, wait," he said, before wrapping her bare thighs tighter around his hips and leading the way to her bedroom.

Once reaching his destination, he set her feet down near the foot of the bed before laying on the bed, looking up at her and biting his lips seductively. He stared at her hard, watching her watch his erect dick. Long, hard and calling her name.

She already knew what he wanted. It was his favorite sex position and she couldn't lie and say that she didn't like it too. Once he had wrapped up with the condom that she gave him from her nearby drawer, Anika quickly climbed on to her bed, before holding on to his big dick and lowering herself on to him.

Jamal Coleman was her weakness and she wanted him to be hers forever. Wifey would just have to fuck off because Jamal didn't belong to her no more.

Anika would make sure of it.

CHAPTER 4 ~ DARK SECRETS

Lord knows she hated researching for shit.

It's not like she didn't want to get this done - she did. Lord knows that she definitely did. Being free from Leek needed to be done sooner than later, not later. She couldn't continue to stay with this man and expect her future husband to stay with her.

"Mas, your son misses you. Don't you baby?"

Masika annoyingly rolled her eyes and sighed deeply before looking up from her bright laptop screen, only to stare at her mother who sat across the room, on her beige loveseat sofa with her feet up on her cushioned foot stool. Next to her sat Tarique, Masika's three-year-old son who she loved with all her heart, even though she didn't show it as well as she should have.

To say that he didn't look like his father would be a lie. A big fat lie that Masika knew she would have to rectify as soon as it came out her mouth. Tarique was the spitting image of his father. He had inherited all his looks and absolutely none of hers. From those striking green eyes, smooth light skin complexion and that smart mouth of his, Tarique was his father's mini me.

"Mom, don't start," Masika groaned before concentrating on her laptop screen. Searching for a divorce attorney to help her sort out her situation with Leek needed to be done as soon as possible. Masika couldn't waste a single minute anymore being lazy, or else Blaze wouldn't be happy.

"Missh you mommy," Tarique admitted truthfully. Even at three with his speaking skills still a learning process, Tari could express how he felt.

"I know baby. But Mom's just been busy lately, but I promise to make things up to you real soon."

"Don't believe your mama Tari, she's a damn liar," Masika's mom informed him honestly, infuriating Masika completely.

"Mom, you must be forgetting who pays the bills 'round here. You better watch how you talk before the park bench becomes your new bed," Masika threatened firmly, no longer as focused on her laptop screen as she was before. "I apologize for the broken promises Tari but I will make an effort more often. Just give me a few days to sort a few things out, 'kay?"

Tarique said nothing and just sulked, looking down at his hands. Masika didn't mean to always break her promises to her son. Things just came up all the time for her, and she found herself needing to do things for her first, then him. It wasn't intentional… Things just happened.

"Tari, go to your room baby, I need to speak to grandma real quick."

Once Tarique had left the room, Masika wasted no time in telling her mother how she felt about her constantly bringing up some bullshit about how her son missed her.

"You need to cut that shit out, Mom," she snapped irritated. "I already feel bad for leaving him here with you, but chill with the comments all the damn time."

"No you don't," her mother said with a chuckle. "Stop lying to yourself girl. You know you love leaving him here and Lord knows you ain't ever gon' stop."

"Don't worry; soon he'll be out of your hair."

"How? You can't take him anywhere but to his dad's."

"Well, soon I'll be married to my man and he'll be willing to have our son living with us," Masika announced with a delighted grin.

"The same man that knows nothing about your three-year-old?" her mother queried with a smirk. "Yeah, maybe in your dreams chile."

Masika's grin quickly faded and she found herself suddenly irritated with her mother. Usually she would pick an argument with her and send her emotions running through the roof, but today Masika didn't see the point in wasting her energy on her mother.

The only thing she needed to waste her energy on today was finding a divorce attorney. So Masika quickly ignored her mom's presence and got back on the job of finding a divorce attorney.

It didn't take long to stumble upon one of the best in Atlanta. *Jamal Coleman.*

Just reading his biography and all the awards he had achieved had Masika convinced that he was the one to help. He was the best in Atlanta, very fine too, and never lost a divorce case. Masika didn't hesitate in finding his contact details because she was positive that this was the solution to all her problems. Ten minutes later, she was dialing Jamal's office number and silently praying that his assistant picked up sooner than later.

That divorce from Leek was happening as soon as possible, and Masika couldn't wait. And there would be no telling of Tarique to Blaze right now; some secrets were just best being left in the dark for a little while longer.

CHAPTER 5 ~ SEXY STRANGER

~ 3 Weeks Later ~

White Louboutins or the black Louboutins? Masika couldn't seem to make a decision fast enough and she knew that any minute now she would hear a knock on her door, signaling for her to be ready to get the hell out of her house. *The white ones would go better with my lilac two-piece though,* Masika mused to herself before deciding that her white designer shoes would do just the trick.

Thankfully, five minutes later, Masika had yet to hear a knock on her door, which surprised her but also relaxed her. At least she had more time to look sexy for her man before he came to pick her up. Today was a big day not just for her, but for Blaze too.

Masika had finally got in contact with Attorney Coleman himself and explained briefly why she needed his help. However, over the phone wasn't enough to explain all she needed from him. So three weeks later when the phone call came from his assistant about their meeting today, Masika was over the moon. This didn't mean that she was no longer going to be Leek's wife by the end of today, but it was a start. A start that would lead to her great victory.

Finally, Masika's doorbell rang and a smile instantly grew on her lips once she went to her door and answered it.

There in all his glory stood her sexy thug. She wasn't really paying attention to his clothes swag, as all she could see was that handsome chocolate face, those mesmerizing grey eyes and those thick lips. But her man looked good rocking a causal white tee with two large gold chains, sweatpants and white J's on his feet.

"Baby, you ready?" he queried with a smirk before taking a step closer to her, looking up and down at her lustfully. "You lookin' so fuckin' sexy bae..." At 6'3", he towered over her and made her feel so protected and loved. Just looking up into those grey eyes, was always a panty wetter for Masika.

"I'm ready," she said sexily with a nod before grabbing his strong bicep and moving closer to steal a kiss from him.

Blaze was loving the way she was looking right now and as she branded their lips together, his hands moved from her curvy waist to her ass covered by her lilac bodycon skirt. He squeezed her soft cheeks tightly before spanking them hard.

A soft moan escaped her lips between the passionate kiss, and Blaze continued to enjoy the sweet taste of her cherry lipstick before quickly pulling away. "Go get in the car," he ordered firmly. "Before I fuck yo' pretty ass on this door 'til you can't think straight." Masika was really loving every sound of his aggressive but sexy words, and would gladly have her man on her apartment door right now but unfortunately, duty called first.

Thirty minutes later, Blaze had driven Masika in his red Lambo all the way to their destination. Now here they sat, hand in hand and waiting patiently in Attorney Coleman's waiting room. His assistant had assured Masika that in a few minutes Coleman would be ready to meet her. Masika didn't mind too much about waiting, she just really wanted to get this shit over and done with. It had been eating away at her for two months now. Never in her life would she have figured that she would need a divorce this desperately.

"Babe, I need to pee," Masika revealed to Blaze coolly before giving him a quick peck on his left cheek.

"A'ight," Blaze nodded at her watching as she got up out her seat. He couldn't help but stare straight at her fat ass. He was loving the way it looked so juicy in that tight skirt of hers. He couldn't wait to get all up in that when they got back to her place. Once receiving directions to the restroom from Attorney Coleman's assistant, Masika was gone, leaving Blaze in his seat. He resulted to bringing out his iPhone and playing a quick game of Candy Crush, shrugging off the feeling of someone watching him.

But he was absolutely right to think that someone was watching him because she couldn't keep her eyes off him. He hadn't noticed her properly when he had first arrived, which made her feel sort of invisible. His main concern was the girl right next to him, dressed in a revealing but classy lilac two-piece bodycon skirt and crop top. *His* girl. Anika couldn't help but feel slightly envious at the fact that he seemed so focused on his girlfriend, nothing else or nobody else.

3.47pm.

Anika took another peek at the sexy specimen of a man sitting across from her and then dropped her eyes to the paperwork on her desk, willing herself not to look again. But it was hard as hell. He was sitting right across from her, waiting for his girlfriend to return to his side. Although he wasn't doing anything but staring at the screen of his cell phone, it was something about his aura that pulled her in…and not just her. Other women in the waiting room had been stealing glances as well, before they went on their merry way out.

Shifting in her seat, Anika looked up one more time and allowed her eyes to linger on the man sitting across from her desk, for what she was telling herself, was the last time. He was still staring at his cell phone, so she took the opportunity to let her eyes slowly inspect every inch of him. He had clear, caramel skin and a chiseled jawline with light facial hair that formed a perfectly lined-up goatee. His hair was cut low but he had soft waves that swirled around and gave him a pretty boy look. But it was obvious that he wasn't a pretty boy. He was dressed in sweatpants and a simple white tee with all white J's on his feet. And he was wearing two large gold chains, a flashy gold Rolex and a diamond stud on each ear; this swagged out man had money, no doubt about it.

Damn, Anika thought to herself as she went back to his plump lips and focused in.

Then, while she was looking, he flicked his pink tongue out of his mouth and licked his lips slowly. Call it attraction or sexual frustration from the fact that she hadn't had any in a while, Anika nearly creamed at the sight. She tore her attention away from his lips and then looked right into his grey eyes. He winked and she panicked. He was staring right at her.

Oh shit! Anika thought to herself as she lowered her eyes back to the papers on her desk and covered her face with her hands. She could feel her cheeks grow hot with embarrassment. He had caught her right in the act of eye-raping his body.

"So yo' pretty ass don't speak?"

His question caught her by surprise. He knew it too because once she turned to stare at him, he could see the surprise in her pretty brown eyes.

Fuck, she is gorgeous! Blaze thought to himself.

Yeah, he was engaged but that didn't mean he couldn't look. Shit, he wasn't blind. As long as he didn't touch, Blaze knew Masika wouldn't be gunning for his ass.

As Blaze watched her struggle for a response, he had to chuckle to himself. This wouldn't be the first time that his aggressive nature had caught a woman off guard, but it was the first time that it had happened to a woman so beautiful. She was acting all embarrassed and shit like a nigga had never spoke game to her before. It was such a sharp contrast from Masika who was a hood chick and used to niggas trying to talk shit to her. She always had a good comeback waiting for anything someone tried to say. Not like this chick.

He took a minute to admire her look. She had long, wavy dark brown hair and the way it cascaded around her, made her seem like a goddess that he needed to please. Those red lips that he wanted to kiss and feel on every part of his body. That cute button nose of hers that he wanted to rub his own against and that perfect light skin of hers that made him want to massage lotion over her day and night.

Man, you gotta stop this shit. You engaged now, he tried to tell himself. But one more look at her and he ignored his own warning.

"I do speak," she responded shyly, surprised at how deep his baritone sounded. It was a voice so smooth, so sexy that made her heat up with excitement, and feel a small pool in her panties. "I'm just waiting for your fiancée to come back so I can escort you both to Attorney Coleman's office."

"Well, she probably takin' a shit," he commented amusingly, grinning widely and showcasing his pearly whites.

Anika kept silent at his crude words, rolled her eyes, and focused her attention back on her computer screen.

The atmosphere became slightly awkward and tense until Blaze decided that he wanted to break the ice with this pretty lady. "I'm Blaze," he introduced himself friendly.

Blaze...What an interesting name for an interesting man, Anika couldn't help but ponder in her private thoughts. *Obviously a nickname.*

"Anika," she said quickly, not bothering to look back at him. She didn't want to fall into the trap of letting those grey eyes win her over again.

"That's a real pretty name, ma'," he complimented her sweetly.

She felt her cheeks becoming hotter and even as she tried to stop herself blushing, she couldn't help it. Being light skinned definitely didn't help hide her blushing away from him.

"Thank you."

"No proble-"

Just before Blaze could finish his sentence, in came walking in Masika, very annoyed. She stood right in front of Anika, blocking her view of Blaze completely and threw her hands on her hips.

"Why didn't you tell me the restrooms were bein' cleaned? I had to wait twenty minutes for that rude ass lady to finish cleaning, then to make matters worse, she ain't even clean the damn place very well!"

The cleaning woman, Simona, always did an excellent job. That's why Anika convinced Attorney Coleman to hire her in the first place. Masika must have been tripping just because she had to wait.

"I apologise, Ms Brooks. Please let me escort you and your fiancé to Attorney Coleman's office," Anika instructed gently as she stood up and smoothed down her black pencil skirt.

Masika rolled her eyes and sighed softly before reaching for Blaze's hand once he walked up beside her. Looking down briefly, Anika noticed that as soon as Masika reached for his hand, he didn't hold on to hers. He just let her hand linger on his and kept his grey eyes on Anika. Concealing a smirk, Anika turned around to lead them into the attorney's office. *Stop it Anika... He's engaged.*

But Anika couldn't help the way she suddenly felt about this fine nigga. Call it whatever you liked, but Anika was definitely feeling Blaze and she had a feeling that he was feeling her too.

However, once opening Attorney Coleman's door for Blaze and his fiancée, Anika couldn't help but feel a small hint of jealousy at the way Blaze had his arm wrapped lovingly around her curvy waist as they walked in to meet their new attorney.

You see Anika? He's completely taken.

***

As Masika searched in her purse for the documents that Attorney Coleman had asked her to bring, all she kept thinking about was Tarique. And how she was positive that the only way for this whole process to run smoothly was if she sent him away to another state. She couldn't risk Blaze finding out about him anytime soon. And there was no way that she was giving Leek an opportunity to tell Blaze about Tari. *Hell nah!*

As Masika searched in her purse for some important documents and laid them out on the table for Attorney Coleman, all Blaze kept thinking about was that gorgeous goddess sitting behind that desk. He hadn't had the opportunity to inspect her body yet, but that didn't matter right now. All that mattered was that pretty face of hers that he couldn't get out his mind. *Blaze... You need to stop this shit man. You have a woman... A fiancée matter fact!*

Blaze low-key wished he hadn't come with Masika today. He wanted to be the supportive boyfriend that she appreciated and loved. That's why he agreed to follow her. But how was he being supportive when all he could think about was Anika? His mind wasn't even on Attorney Coleman speaking to Masika about the shit she had to do leading up to her court case with Leek. Anika was the only one on his mind and he was even feeling to step out the meeting for a bit, claim he was going to the restroom but really go and speak to Anika. Maybe find out more about her, her full name, her interes-

Fuck no! Blaze quickly ran his palm over his face, trying his hardest to concentrate and forget about her. There was no point in focusing on a woman that wasn't his and probably already taken.

***

"So my god mother's barbeque is this weekend and you already promised to come so no excuses hun."

Anika sighed softly as she pictured him in nothing but his white Calvin Klein boxers and completely dripping from head to toe in water. Those muscles, those abs... Lord, he was trying to kill her! She could see his hard dick print bulging out his boxers, beckoning her to come closer and get exactly what she desired. His grey eyes continued to eye fuck her. Those cute dimples of his revealed themselves, as he smirked sexily at her before he looked down between his legs and tightly grabbed his dick. His head shot back up as he asked her, *"This what'chu want?"* She slowly nodded, biting her lips shyly. *"Then come fuckin' get it baby,"* he ordered firmly before adding, *"It's all yours... Just come a lil' closer and get all this big dic-"*

"Anika!"

Anika blinked rapidly, immediately snapping herself out of her naughty daydream. Why couldn't she stop thinking about this complete stranger? A handsome, mysterious and cocky stranger.

"Were you even listening to what I said?" Sadie queried, watching her suspiciously.

"Yeah," Anika nodded trying to reassure her. "Your god mother's barbeque. This weekend. I'll be there."

"Good. Don't be late," Sadie stated with a satisfied smirk. "Now what had you so distracted just now girl?"

"Nothing, I'm just tired, honestly."

"Hmmm... Anika Scott tired? Since when? You never seem to get tired of Jamal Coleman's dick."

Anika frowned at her slightly before responding, "See that's the thing... I never seem to get tired of him but it looks like he's getting tired of me."

"What makes you say that?"

"We haven't had sex in three weeks Sadie," Anika revealed sadly.

"Seriously?"

"And you know I'm not the type to pressure a man, but he hasn't made any sort of intimacy with me. He just keeps treating me like... like..."

"Like?"

"His assistant."

Even though that's exactly what she was to Jamal, Anika couldn't just let all that they had shared together go down the drain. She had stopped her whole dating game - for him. Stopped going the extra mile for other men when going out to the club - for him. But now he was treating her like a common employee, when she clearly wasn't.

"Maybe he's decided to become celibate," Sadie suggested gently.

"No Sadie," Anika quickly disagreed. Jamal couldn't become celibate. He loved pussy way too much. "He's not celibate. I think he's sorting things out."

"With the wife?"

Anika nodded with a roll of her eyes and a groan. "I hate her, I hate her, I hate her! Why can't she just fuck off and leave Jamal for me? She doesn't treat him well, so it only makes sense if he's with me."

"Hun... Maybe this is a sign for you," Sadie said truthfully.

"A sign? What kind of sign?"

"A sign for you to move on from him."

"No... No, it can't be," Anika snapped.

"Just think about it," Sadie offered softly. "He's been fucking you for months, telling you all sorts of things, but after it all he's still with her. Even though you've held him down better than her, he's still with her, not you."

Anika took a deep breath as she listened to her best friend's true words. She had a point. A big point. Through it all Jamal was still with his wifey, and he never once made a move to leave her. He just kept by her side. It was as if he was never leaving her, and just playing Anika this whole time.

***

As Kareem and Marquise debated over what had happened and who was getting punished first, Blaze contemplated on Masika's words to him before he left her tonight.

"Babe... I can't go to your auntie's barbeque this weekend. I got an e-mail from Attorney Coleman's assistant and she told me another meeting has been scheduled. I don't want you to miss the barbeque baby, so don't worry about attending the meeting with me. I'll see if I can make it later though?"

It was funny because Blaze didn't really care about the fact that she wasn't coming. What he cared about was the fact that she had received an e-mail directly from Anika and all he could think about was what he would do if he had her e-mail.

Man, stop this shit man, Blaze tried to convince himself to get his mind on more pressing matters. *You don't need no other woman. You already got the baddest bitch holding you down.*

"Whoever did this shit has to die man," Kareem snapped with a fist bang to the glass table.

"I agree, ain't nobody ever had the audacity to attack our trap house and steal from us too? Those motherfuckers are askin' to die now," Marquise intervened as he sucked his teeth rudely. "We can't allow this to lie B'."

"And we won't," Blaze finally spoke, sitting up straight in his chair as he looked at his right-hand men that sat in front of him. "What's the word on who did this shit?"

Blaze couldn't believe it once he heard the news. Someone had actually plucked up the courage to come for his empire. Someone was playing with fire and Blaze was going to make sure that the fire burned them severely.

"We got word from the Scorpios that it's the Lyons," Kareem revealed simply.

"And we all know exactly who runs the Lyons," Marquise stated with a large frown. "That motherfucker is a dead man."

Just from the mere mention of the Lyons had Blaze irritated. Only because the Lyons was run by a man that Blaze couldn't fuck with. Not now not ever. The very mention of his name had Blaze irritated, making him wanting to punch or hit something. It didn't help that Masika happened to be married to the fool.

Leek Carter.

"Just say the word B' and we end that fool," Marquise reassured Blaze, as he leaned forward on the glass table and stared seriously at Blaze.

"The amount of damage he caused... Man I swear he's gon' get it. We gon' get our shit back off him too," Kareem added sternly.

"We gotta do something fast too, niggas gon' think we soft all of a sudden and don't do shit," Marquise voiced worriedly.

Blaze was fully aware of what Leek and his boys had set up. They had stupidly decided to hit one of their trap houses up north. Not only had they shot all men on sight and burned the building, they had taken money and some of the finest Colombian dope that Blaze and his team had to offer. Their connect, Sergio had hooked them up constantly with the finest product, and stocked them with all the ammo they needed to stay protected. All they had to do was make those stacks of green for him and everybody was happy.

Unfortunately for the Knight Nation, they had been caught slipping and this definitely wasn't a good look. Blaze knew that Leek's punishment would have to be severe in order to make sure that he was dealt with and learnt his lesson. Fuck the fact that he was still married to Masika. Blaze didn't give a shit.

"Don't worry boys," Blaze informed his boys with a small grin. "We're the fuckin' Knight Nation, we got this all under control. The Lyons know they fucked up messin' with us and they know we comin' for all their dumb asses. Just chill. They're mice, we're cats. We'll catch them slippin' one by one, and make sure they never forget who the fuck we are."

Kareem and Marquise's faces instantly brightened up after Blaze's bold words. Blaze knew he had his boys assured that this shit wasn't over. He was going to ensure that the Lyons got exactly what they truly deserved, especially that stupid nigga Leek.

CHAPTER 6 ~ SURPRISE MEETINGS

There was no way that Masika was going to follow Blaze to his auntie's barbeque. She didn't feel like kicking it with any of his family, when she knew they didn't like her. Fuck trying to make them like her. She liked herself, Blaze loved her and that's all that mattered.

Masika gently giggled as her nail technician lifted her feet out the warm water and quickly began scrubbing. She couldn't help but giggle, she was a ticklish female especially when it involved her feet.

"Girl, how'd your meeting go?"

Masika turned her head to her side to stare into Desiree's dark blue eyes. Masika knew how much of a fan her sister was when it came to contact lenses. She claimed she hated looking at her boring brown eyes that almost every black person on earth had. Contact lenses made things fun and exciting, adding more to her personality. Both twenty-six and both born with similar personalities, Masika and Desiree were the closest of sisters.

"Good," Masika responded with a small smile. "Attorney Coleman's being a great help and completely focused on getting my divorce finalized."

"Sounds like things are going well. How's Tari?"

"He's cool," Masika replied nonchalantly. "He's staying with mom, but I'm moving him with Auntie Jo in a few days."

"Auntie Jo, who lives in Florida?" Desiree queried with an arch of her perfect brow. "Why you moving him?"

"Because."

"Because what?"

"I haven't told Blaze about him yet..." Masika words trailed off quietly as she shut her eyes trying to relax and stay calm.

"Woah... Seriously sis, it's been two years and you're still keeping this secret away from him?" Desiree questioned her firmly. "You need to tell him about Tari already."

Masika exhaled deeply before looking down at the petite Korean lady tending to her feet and quickly shooed her away. Once the lady was out of sight, Masika spoke. "And I will Des," she said simply. "Just not now."

"Why not?"

"I need to marry him first and have a place in his home. Once that's done, I tell him all about Tari."

"But don't you think it'll be too late then Mas... He's gonna be so angry with yo-"

Masika cut her off rudely. "When I'm his wife? I don't think so. He'll get over it and learn to love Tari with time. But there's no way that I can tell him now. Let's just keep things the way they are for now... then I'll tell him. So let's just stop talking 'bout it, 'kay?"

Masika stared at her pretty sister waiting for her to respond to her request. With her smooth caramel skin, thick thighs, small waist, big breasts but small ass, Desiree had always been known to be a bad bitch. Masika knew she could count on her sister to continue to keep her mouth shut and keep her secret, a secret, for a little while longer.

Desiree reluctantly nodded before looking away from her sister, trying to hide her disappointment and anger. She hated the fact that Masika had stolen her man and was still with him, despite the fact that she was still married and had a secret child too! But for Masika, things were going to change and Desiree was going to make sure of it.

Fuck the fact that they were sisters. That definitely didn't mean shit anymore ever since Masika had stolen Blaze away from Desiree. Desiree knew that Masika must have forgotten about the fact that the only reason why she had met Blaze two years ago in her apartment was because he had just got done fucking Desiree. Then she had the audacity to let Blaze have her number and take her out. Desiree always knew that her sister was one greedy bitch, but for her to steal Blaze was disrespectful. And Desiree wasn't going to let things lie still. Desiree was going to make sure that Masika's secrets revealed themselves to Blaze whether she liked it or not. Secrets left in the dark were always going to be brought back out into the light and exposed... eventually.

***

You look good girl, Anika told herself as she ran her fingers through her curly hair once more and decided that one more coat of red lipstick would do just the trick. But just as she reached into her purse to get it, Ice Cube's voice sounded through her Mercedes-Benz SUV telling her that it was time to get the hell out her car, or her best friend was going to crucify her.

Straight outta Compton, crazy motherfucker named Ice Cube.
From the gang called Niggaz With Attitu-

"Hey gurl," Anika greeted her friend warmly, smiling at her pretty reflection in her car's mirror, tilting it to face her better.

"Where you at? Everyone's here except your late ass," Sadie complained loudly in her ear.

"I'm just getting out my car hun, chill out, I'll be there in thirty seconds."

"You better be," Sadie stated with a rude suck of her teeth before hanging up the call.

Anika couldn't help but chuckle at her best friend's cold demeanor towards her slightly late arrival. She knew she would have to make it up to her as soon as she stepped through the door. Anika took one last look at her reflection, smiling happily and stepping out her car to head to the barbeque inside.

As soon as she got to the brown door and went to press the white doorbell, the door immediately swung open and Anika felt her hands being pulled, dragging her into the sweet cinnamon scented home. She didn't even get a chance to properly admire the modern themed decorated, three-story home, but as Sadie continued pulling her through to the garden, she noticed topaz colored walls, the neatly arranged furniture, and the polished mahogany flooring that her Louboutins kept clicking on.

Once they finally made it to the garden, the funky sounds of Will Smith's "Summertime" filled her eardrums, suddenly making her feel at home.

"I'm so glad you're here Nika!" Sadie exclaimed happily, grabbing hold of her hips and hugging her. Anika accepted the warm hug, glad to see her best friend no longer in a cold mood now that she had arrived. "You look real good girl... And there's a ton of fine single guys here. Just choose your pick."

Sadie let go and came to stand right beside her, linking arms with her before grinning. "Everyone," Sadie announced loudly to the various people sitting down eating, playing card games, standing up dancing, grabbing drinks and small cute kids running up and down playing. "Meet my beautiful best friend, Anika!"

Anika nervously smiled at Sadie's relatives, feeling quite shy as all eyes were on her. But nothing compared to how she felt when her wandering eyes landed straight on his grey ones. She had to blink a few times to convince herself that this was a dream. *He* wasn't here right now. This was dream… Had to be…Right?

Oh shit...oh shit...oh shit! It wasn't a dream. Her heart almost stopped and her knees felt weak as she watched him, watching her. Wait...What the hell was he doing here? Anika wanted to faint, that's how shocked she was. And with the way he was glaring at her she knew he was just as shocked to see her here. But once that pink tongue of his sexily flicked across his thick lips, Anika was a goner. Blaze, the sexy stranger was here in the flesh and his fiancée nowhere in sight.

Blaze almost had to do a double take once he saw her. Fuck, she looked gorgeous! She was rocking a baby pink knee-high dress that had a low neck line revealing some of her tempting cleavage and clung to her killer curves lovingly. Blaze couldn't help but lick his lips at her Coke bottle figure. With those seductive long legs, perfect sized tits, curves and flat stomach - Blaze was infatuated. And when she turned around to go get some food with Sadie, his god cousin, he had to quickly use his hand to cover the sudden hard on he had grown watching her ass move. *Damn!* It was the perfect size and shape, making him want to creep up behind her and feel it. *What the fuck are you thinking man?* Blaze questioned himself, irritated. *Stop this shit. Now.*

But even he couldn't ignore his own warning as he continued to watch her for the rest of the barbeque. He noticed everything. The way she talked, ate, sat, danced, laughed and smiled. Call it whatever you liked, Blaze didn't see no harm done by just looking. Anika was an undeniable beauty and he figured she was used to men checking her out all the time. Even a few of his cousins and uncles couldn't stop drooling over her.

Anika couldn't believe how much attention she was receiving from him. And she hadn't even uttered one word to him yet, but still he kept staring at her. Hard. Even she sneaked a peek, noticing how he refused to take those grey eyes off her and winked numerous times, making her crack a small smile every time.

Sadie had revealed to Anika that Blaze was her god cousin. Her god mother was his auntie, making them god cousins. They hardly talked or saw each other than at family functions like this, because he was a very busy man. Since Sadie had lost her mother and father in a car accident at such a young age, her god mother and her family was the only family she really had and cared about.

"Sadie, I'm going to the restroom real quick," Anika informed her best friend.

"Oh okay...you need help finding it?"

"Nah, I'm cool," Anika convinced her, knowing that she was way too caught up in the card game that she was playing with her uncles.

Blaze couldn't help but remember Masika and why she wasn't here. Didn't she say she had a meeting with Attorney Coleman? Blaze found it strange that the meeting was on a Saturday but what bothered him slightly was the fact that Anika, Attorney Coleman's assistant, was here partying at his auntie's barbeque. Shouldn't she have been at work right now? When she got up from her seat, Blaze saw this as the perfect opportunity to follow her and find out why she wasn't at work.

He waited patiently in the corridor leading to the restrooms, for her to come out. He couldn't wait to see the look on her pretty face once she saw him standing by the wall, both eyes on her.

As soon as she stepped out, Anika froze. There he stood, in all his glory, one leg up resting on the wall, hands tucked in both his chino pockets with a smirk on his plump lips. Anika's eyes gently wandered up and down his body inspecting him properly. He looked handsome in a checkered black and white shirt, brown chino pants and fresh Timberlands on his feet. Not to forget that he was wearing a single silver chain, a silver Rolex and a stud in each ear. Those muscles fitted so lovingly into his shirt, making Anika fantasize how she would rub and lick all over his hot body. *God... This man is so fine!*

"Why ain't yo' ass at work?"

His bold question caught her off guard, snapping her out of her dirty thoughts. That deep baritone of his was starting to have a hold on her.

"It's a Saturday," she responded with a confused expression on her pretty face. "I don't work on Saturdays."

"Don't Coleman have a meetin' with Masika today?"

Anika shook her head no before responding. "He doesn't work on Saturdays."

"You sure?" he queried with an arched brow raised with surprise.

"Of course I'm sure," she assured him. "I'm his assistant."

"A'ight Miss Assistant. I believe you," he stated with a smirk. "You enjoyin' the barbeque?"

Before Anika could even get a chance to respond, in came Sadie watching the pair suspiciously.

"What's going on over here?" she asked with a sneaky grin.

"Nothing," Anika announced, dismissing Blaze's presence completely as she began walking towards her best friend. "What's up?"

"Okay... Well," Sadie immediately linked arms with Anika and began leading her down the corridor back to the main house room. Blaze slowly followed behind from a distance, unintentionally overhearing their conversation.

"Since it's a Saturday, your favorite day, I'm thinking we go to your favorite place tonight." Anika's eyes lit up like diamonds after her statement.

"Cheetah Lounge?"

"Yaaass gurl," Sadie confirmed excitedly. "We gotta see Candi tonight!"

Anika couldn't wait to get up out of here. Strip clubs were like her own personal heroin and there wasn't a single person on the planet who could change her mind about the way she felt about them. A dance from Candi would definitely make her sleep real happy tonight.

***

"A'ight... So we got the whereabouts of Leek's right-hand man, Donte," Marquise announced contently.

"I say we go hit up this guy right now. What'chu think B'?" Kareem queried curiously, watching Blaze as he sat peacefully in his driver's seat watching the dark road ahead.

Why the hell would she lie to him? Blaze just didn't understand why Masika would say that she had a meeting with Coleman today when she clearly didn't if the man didn't work on Saturday. And of course his assistant of all people would know that simple fact.

"Blaze… What'chu think man? We doing this shit now or what?" Kareem's question managed to snap Blaze's attention away from Masika. He would just have to think about her lying ass some other time. Right now, he had business to take care off.

"We doin' this shit now," Blaze affirmed firmly. "After we sort the fool, we're going out to celebrate. One down, only a few more to go."

"Sounds like a plan," Marquise stated excitedly before adding, "Where we goin' to celebrate though?"

Blaze paused momentarily, contemplating to himself before speaking with a smirk, "Cheetah Lounge."

CHAPTER 7 ~ CHEETAH LOUNGE

I got two bitches twerkin', screamin' that's my best friend
(her best friend)
Oh you better, you better, you better (girl)
I got two bitches twerkin', screamin' that's my best friend
(her best friend)
Oh you better
You want her back? Then come and get her
And her best friend

As soon as Candi hit the stage, Anika and Sadie excitedly got up from their front row seats and began dropping all their dollar bills on her as she twerked in front of them. Anika loved everything about the way Candi moved. It wasn't just about the fact that the girl had some real, amazing skills; it was also about the fact that Candi was one bad ass chick! Everyone who came to Cheetah Lounge always requested for Candi, and ballers, even bachelors were always eager to pay top dollar for her alone. Candi had a fat ass that not a single soul in the room could miss. With that fat ass came killer curves, a smooth toffee complexion, full lips, thirty-two inches of the best silk Peruvian weave and thick, long legs that could gracefully wrap around that glittery golden pole.

"Yaassss Candi," Anika shouted ecstatically as she continued to watch Candi twerking while doing a split on the spotlight stage and happily threw more bills onto her.

Cheetah Lounge was a strip club like no other. Each night, the club was given a theme and decorated accordingly. Tonight was

The Great Gatsby theme, and each of the dancers were dressed in flashy, sparkly and striking lingerie giving them all a classy but seductive look with white feather boas hanging around their necks. The entire club was decorated with gold chandeliers, gold tables and gold chairs, and the only drinks being served tonight were strictly champagne and vodka.

"Shake that pretty ass girl!" Sadie exclaimed, slapping Candi's ass with a large stack of dollar bills. Candi turned around to stare at Anika and Sadie, her hazel eyes lit up like diamonds before giving the ladies both a sexy wink. Then she turned back around to face the stripper pole and dancing exactly the way they wanted her to.

An hour later, Candi was off the stage and Anika and Sadie decided to make their way to the bar. Now that Candi was done for the night, Anika didn't see the point of hanging around at the club no more. Candi was her only favourite stripper. It wasn't just about the way she moved, it was the way she brought personality to the stage and owned the room.

"Hun, I gotta go to the restroom real quick. Then we'll go," Sadie informed Anika gently, taking one last sip of her champagne before quickly rushing off to the nearest restroom.

Anika sighed softly as she watched the current stripper on the stage. Yeah, she was talented but not as talented as Candi. As far as Anika was concerned, none of the other strippers at Cheetah Lounge had a thing on Candi. Anika lifted her champagne glass to her lips and allowed the sweet substance to run on her tongue, relaxing her. She couldn't wait to get home and relax properly in a nice, warm bath.

When Sadie finally arrived back to the bar, she had the biggest smile on her lips that had Anika a little confused. What could have happened over the five minutes that she had been gone?

"Guess what girl!"

"What?" Anika queried curiously, wanting to know what was up with Sadie's sudden happiness.

"We're meeting Candi backstage! Right now!" Sadie revealed cheerfully, grabbing Anika's arm as she jumped up and down.

Anika almost fainted on the spot. "What do you mean we're meeting Candi backstage? How?!"

"I met the owner of the club backstage. Turns out I know him," Sadie voiced blissfully. "He's giving us free access backstage to meet her!"

"Oh my gosh!" Anika's shock and excitement couldn't conceal itself. And things only continued to get better and better for her once they were standing in Candi's personal dressing room and admiring her, as she counted the money she made tonight.

"I hear y'all gorgeous gurls are my biggest fans," Candi's thick Southern accent sounded through the room, building Anika's excitement as she was hearing Candi's voice for the very first time.

"You're a true goddess Candi, we love you," Sadie informed her calmly.

"Yes!" Anika voiced loudly. "Absolutely! You're amazingly talented, beautiful and confident. I love everything about you! Especially the way you move on stage." Anika couldn't hold it in. She just had to tell Candi what she thought about her. Candi seemed to be loving her words too because a large smile grew on her pink lips, revealing her pearly whites.

"Thank you, thank you," she responded softly. "I appreciate y'all for coming backstage to meet me and tell me what y'all think."

Anika couldn't help but continue to admire this bad ass female sitting in front of her. Her favorite stripper in the entire city of Atlanta was thanking her for stating her opinion about her. This night was only seeming to get better and better for Anika.

"Y'all are welcome here anytime you like," Candi revealed warmly. "Don't hesitate to come and kick it with me. It'll be fun to give y'all a private show too."

"That sounds wonderful," Anika stated truthfully and Sadie nodded enthusiastically next to her.

"Make sure y'all get your access passes from B' before you leave," Candi instructed simply. "It'll let you come through backstage whenever you like. And next time you come through you'll get a grand tour by yours truly."

Anika was loving the sound of everything that Candi was saying, but there was one thing that had popped up that was now bugging her.

"Is B' the owner?" Anika queried curiously, watching Candi's gorgeous reflection in the glass mirror.

Candi nodded quickly before replying, "B's the owner of Cheetah Lounge. He hates it when I call him that, but I'm the only one who he allows to do it."

"Oh, why does he hate it?" Anika questioned.

"Because it's not his full name, it's just an initial. An initial only his boys get to call him."

They say curiosity killed the cat, but curiosity only fueled Anika's desire to find out more about the mysterious owner of the Cheetah Lounge who had let her and Sadie backstage, free of charge.

"Oh I see... And what's his full name? Do you know?"

"Yeah I do," Candi nodded knowingly before adding, "It's Bl-"

"It's Blaze," said a sudden deep baritone voice from behind, cutting Candi off completely.

It wasn't even the mention of his name from Candi that had Anika shocked. It was the smooth sound of that deep voice that Anika hadn't been able to shake off or stop thinking about that had her more surprised. And the fact that Sadie had failed to reveal nothing.

Anika slowly turned around only to stare nervously at the sexy stranger she had seen a few hours ago at his auntie's barbeque. He was leaning against the open door, both hands deep in his pockets and his eyes darting up and down on her appearance.

Fuck, he looks so hot! Anika wanted nothing more than to run up to him and feel those big hands moving up and down her body. All she could do was stare in awe as those grey eyes glared back at her lustfully. The way he was watching her had her feeling some type of way. Some type of freaky way. Those grey eyes were definitely going to be the death of her.

This was all her fault. He couldn't keep his damn eyes off her the entire night. And watching her throw all those dollar bills on Candi made him more fascinated with her. Seeing her happy, made him happy and he didn't really understand why. Why'd she have to be so fucking attractive?

Now here they stood. Watching each other lustfully and keeping nothing but silent. Even though he had seen her at the barbeque already, her outfit still looked so new, better and fresh to his eyes. That tight dress of hers looked even sexier than it had before. It complemented her body well and Blaze badly wanted to be the one to strip it off her body tonight. *Yo... The fuck you thinking right now?*

"Lemme holla at'chu real quick ma'," Blaze requested, directly talking to Anika and cutting off the loud silence that had developed.

"You wanna talk to me cuzzo?" Sadie queried, clearly confused.

"Nah, not you," he informed her gently. "You," he voiced firmly, pointing at Anika. He observed as her brown eyes widened with surprise, and she nervously bit her bottom lip before slowly stepping forward and following him outside Candi's dressing room.

Once outside, Blaze watched as she began distancing herself away from him, clearly trying her hardest not to stand too close. Blaze found it amusing that he was having such an effect on her. He didn't even wanna talk to her anymore. Shit, he didn't even really have anything legit to say. All he wanted to do was stare into those innocent brown pools of hers, without making it awkward with others around.

The way he continued to stare at her was starting to make her feel slightly intimidated. This handsome man was the owner of the

Cheetah Lounge and the reason for why she had just met Candi. She needed to say something. A 'thank you', or a simple 'what do you want' would suffice. She chose the first option.

"Thank you for letting us meet Candi," she said quietly, still unable to pull her eyes away from his.

"No problem," he responded with a smirk. "I saw how yo' wild ass acted 'round her." A light laugh escaped his lips, and Anika couldn't help but begin to blush at the fact that he had seen her frantically and happily throwing dollar bills. "You come here all the time?"

"Mostly weekends," she stated. "And whenever I'm having a boring or bad day."

Blaze nodded at her before becoming silent again. He didn't understand why she was having such a huge effect on his behavior right now. Blaze was feeling nervous and being a thug, Blaze was never one to feel nervous. *Masika ain't even had me feeling like this before... I don't believe this shit.*

"Why'd you bring me out here?" Anika queried curiously, snapping Blaze out his private thoughts.

Why'd you bring her out here Blaze? To stare at her some more? You gotta stop this soppy, shy crap man.

"I just wan' say thank you," he stated calmly, thinking fast on his feet of some type of excuse.

"For what?"

"For helpin' Attorney Coleman with Masika's case," Blaze told her confidently.

"I'm just his assistant, I don't do much but take his calls, fix hi-"

Blaze interrupted her, "You still help the nigga with his cases right?"

"Yeah, but I'm no-"

"And that's why I'm thankin' you," he pushed.

"But I don't do much real-"

"Accept it, Miss Assistant," Blaze ordered her firmly. "I don't usually thank people for shit. So just accept it."

Anika exhaled softly, slightly annoyed but slightly turned on by his aggressive way. "Alright... You're welcome."

"I think I deserve a little more than just a 'you're welcome' ma'," Blaze announced simply. "After all, I just let you meet the baddest stripper in the lounge, for free."

Anika quickly ran her fingers through her curls, one of the things that she did when she was nervous. Blaze currently had her nerves running through the roof, especially with the way he was looking at her. "And what is it that you deserve?"

"It's up to yo' pretty ass to decide, Miss Assistant," he explained with a smug grin.

"Okay…how about a handshake?" she questioned shyly, knowing it was silly.

Blaze shot her a rude look and she knew that the handshake suggestion was a no go. So she contemplated to herself for a while before deciding that a friendly hug would do.

"A hug?"

Blaze grey eyes immediately lit up like diamonds and he nodded willingly, but still kept still as he leaned against the pink wall. She figured that since she was the one suggesting the hug, she would have to be the one to start it.

Anika took a deep sigh before slowly moving closer to him, having nowhere else to look but at him. When she finally made it in front of him, she stopped and continued to swoon over those grey eyes of his. They couldn't be real, right?

"They're real, Miss Assistant," said Blaze amusingly, answering her private question.

"How did you..." Blaze ignored her and suddenly grabbed onto her curvy waist, wanting to waste no time in getting his hug. "Stop talkin', I want my hug." Watching her make her way to him was enough to make him almost bust in his pants.

His firm touch immediately sent shock waves through her body and a fiery sensation began in between her thighs. She quickly lifted her hands to his broad shoulders and wrapped her arms around his neck. Her chin gently rested on his shoulder as she pressed her chest onto his hard one. Once she felt his hands shift behind her waist, allowing his arms to hold her and pull her closer into him, Anika swore she felt heaven. His spicy man scent had her high already and her sweet scent had him completely infatuated.

"Happy now?" she queried innocently.

"Fuck you think?" he asked back cockily, before holding onto her even tighter, pulling her closer to his body allowing her to feel that large armor in the middle of his pants.

Shit... He's carrying some serious damage, Anika mused. *He's starting to drive me even crazier than before.* Anika couldn't deny she wanted this sexy man. Even though she hardly knew him, she felt like they had known each other for years, just yet to meet in person. She wanted him badly. But there was one issue that no matter how hard she tried, she just couldn't shake off...

His engagement to Masika.

CHAPTER 8 ~ UNRAVELLING SECRETS

"Fuck... Keep suckin' it... Just like that girl."
Slurp. Slurp. Slurp.
"It wasn't us Blaze! Please! We're being set u-"
"Shut yo' ass up," Blaze spat, giving him another few hard whips with his black Versace belt. *"Tired of you fuckin' beggin'... when you know... you and yo' crew... fucked up!"* Blaze exclaimed crazily in between his whips before deciding that it was time to end this fool.
"Blaze, please... Don't kill me ma-"
"We know it was yo' crew that robbed us," Kareem announced boldly, interrupting Donte's pleads. *"Stop lyin' man... You just making this shit worse."*
"Shoulda never let yo' homies attack us," Marquise snapped, angrily kicking Donte in the stomach, resulting in him to crouch forward in pain and cough up some more blood.
Due to the whippings from Blaze's belt, punches from Kareem and kicks from Marquise, Donte was covered in bruises, scars and cuts everywhere. He was shirtless too, so the belt, punches and kicks were hitting his chest, face, stomach and back. It didn't faze Blaze though. He deserved all this shit and more.
Donte was a member of the Lyons, Leek's crew. The same crew that Blaze's Knight Nation just didn't fuck with. Matter fact they hated each other. So it made sense for them to try and attack and stupidly leave their signature gang tag *'LYONS RULE'* at the scene of the attacked trap house.

"We endin' this shit now. No more tryin' to come for us. You stupid little niggas way out yo' league anyways, tryna come for us all the damn time," Blaze stated with a smirk, as he lifted the butt of his gun to the side of Donte's bloody head. *"Say night night, nigga."*

Marquise began to chuckle and Blaze turned his head to stare at him. *"Why you laughin' nigga?"*

"You always got some corny shit to say B'," he responded with another chuckle.

Blaze couldn't help but laugh lightly before turning to Kareem, still pressing the butt of his gun hard into the side of Donte's head.

"Yo Reem, you think I always got some corny shit to say?"

"Sometimes nigga... But I guess that's jus' you," he said with a shrug.

"Hmm, I hear you," Blaze stated before turning down to a petrified Donte. *"Donte, you think I always got some corny shit to say?"*

Donte kept silent and just looked up with tears forming in his brown eyes.

"He asked you a fuckin' question boy," Marquise barked, about to deliver a kick to Donte when Blaze stopped him with a firm hand to his chest.

"Chill Marq... He'll answer it in his own time," Blaze announced calmly. *"What'chu got to say Donte? Think I say some corny shit?"*

Donte took a deep breath, blinked a few times before deciding to break his scared silence. *"I don't... know."*

"Take a wild guess nigga," Blaze cajoled him sternly.

Donte sighed deeply before responding, *"No, you ain't got corn-"*

Pow! Pow! Pow!

Donte never got a chance to finish because Blaze had blown his brains out. *"Wrong answer motherfucker,"* Blaze concluded *confidently with a sinister smile. "I always got corny shit to say once in a while."*

Slurp. Slurp. Slurp.

What had happened to Donte two nights ago was on Blaze's mind at a time like this and he didn't understand why. Why was he so distracted while his fiancée was giving him head in his Lambo?

Even with the way she was swirling that talented tongue of hers around his dick and bobbing her head up and down, he was distracted. Her mouth felt so nice and tight around him and with each lick, suck and swirl, Blaze was on cloud nine. However, cloud nine didn't involve Masika. Instead it involved Anika.

He began to imagine that it was her sweet mouth wrapped around his dick and giving him pleasure right now. He wished it was her. So bad! And as his hand pushed Masika's head further down onto his dick, all he could think about was Anika. Hugging her two nights ago in his Cheetah Lounge had only made things worse. He couldn't get her out his fucking mind!

Slurp. Slurp. Slurp.

Her hands twisted up and down the base of his slippery dick, while her mouth handled his top. He was too big for her mouth but she was still being a pro. Keeping a firm grasp at the hard base of his dick, she stroked him while quickly bobbing her head up and down, using her lips to pull hard on his dick. *Slurp. Slurp. Slurp.*

"Fuuck," he murmured, his eyes rolling deep in pleasure. She was driving him crazy, now flicking her warm tongue against the sensitive head of his dick then quickly swirling her tongue around it. Just as the hot rush was beginning to build, she quickly sucked up and down clearly eager to get him to cum in her mouth. Blaze loved how she couldn't speak, because her mouth was full of his dick. He wished it was her pussy full of dick, as she rode him up and down like his own personal cowgirl. That did it for him. Imagining Anika fully naked, tits out, bouncing up and down as she rode his dick had him quickly busting his nut in Masika's mouth.

Five minutes later, Masika had completely wiped the mess off her man's dick and her mouth. While giving him head she couldn't help but notice how disoriented he seemed away from her. Usually when she gave him head, he was more encouraging and slightly more vocal. Today seemed different though.

But nonetheless, Masika had a motive today. She wanted to use this day well. Today was the day she moved into her man's mansion. Living in that little apartment wasn't going to work no more. And with Tarique moving to Florida soon, she needed a new place that Leek wouldn't dare roll up in, demanding to see his son.

"Baby, what are your plans today?" Masika questioned her man lovingly, staring at him as he looked down at his phone.

"The usual," he murmured, clearly preoccupied with the bright screen below him. "Why?"

"Well... I was thinkin' that you and I spend some time together."

"We always spendin' time together Mas," Blaze announced with a sigh. "Ain't you bored?"

"How can I get bored of my fiancé who I love and cherish?" she questioned him wholeheartedly before adding, "I want us to spend the day together Blaze."

"A'ight, doin' what exactly?"

She paused momentarily, thinking of how she was going to word her idea. "Moving my stuff into your house."

Blaze suddenly looked up from his phone and glared at her. He looked angry all of a sudden and like he wanted to curse her the fuck out. But instead he unlocked his car doors.

"I got a lotta shit to do today Mas, I'll come see you later," he informed her simply before moving in to plant a small kiss on her cheek.

Masika didn't get it. Why couldn't she just move in with him now? She didn't want to wait no more. Why couldn't they address things and start acting more like a married couple?

Reluctantly, Masika kept silent and smiled weakly at him before stepping out his car. Her fiancé was starting to piss her off about their whole living situation. And with every step towards her apartment door, Masika knew that she needed to take control of this situation. One way or another she was moving her shit into his mansion.

***

When you wake up before you brush your teeth
You grab your strap, nigga
Only time you get down on your knees
Shooting craps, nig-

Blaze cut his engine off once he was satisfied with the way he had parked. He got out his car, locking it smoothly with one click of his key button, before quickly heading towards the entrance door of the salon.

Once inside, all eyes were immediately on him. As he strolled through, he noticed the receptionist flashing him a shy smile, a few ladies under the dryer fixing their cleavage and hairdressers turning their necks to see him walk through. "Hey Blaze," the receptionist greeted him warmly. He gave her a head nod and kept it moving. The sudden attention never phased him. Women always seemed to be so damn extra when it came to getting his attention.

It didn't take him long to reach his destination. Once outside the golden oak door, Blaze pushed right through not bothering to knock.

"Malik, what I tell your ass about knocking before entering?"

"Aunt, what I tell yo' ass about callin' me by my government name?"

"Boy don't make me beat your butt."

Blaze couldn't help but laugh at his Auntie Ari as she sat on her leopard print sofa, her feet up while watching the bright plasma screen in front of her.

He instantly plopped right next to her, kissing her forehead and smiling at her cheekily.

"Yo' barbeque was nice. When the next one?" he questioned her curiously, wanting to know if he was getting another opportunity to see Anika.

"Firstly..." his Auntie paused momentarily, waiting for him to scoot closer next to her before she delivered a hard slap to the back of his head.

"Ow!" Blaze groaned in annoyance. "What the hell..."

"That's for not knocking before you enter my Queendom," she retorted with a frown. "What if I was masturbatin' or some shit? Where's your manners boy?"

All Blaze could do was laugh at his crazy auntie. She was crazy, petite, and had a short fuse but he loved her. She was the only person who he had been able to call a mother, ever since he had lost his at the age of seven to breast cancer. The only woman who he felt comfortable around to let down his 'thuggish' guard down. Auntie Ari was the woman who had taken in her sister's son, helped him cope with his mother's death and raising him like her own son. Blaze saw her more as a sister than an auntie. But then, he also saw her as a mother. She was everything he needed her to be and for that he would always be grateful for her. He helped her start her own salon and now here she was five years later, the owner of one of the finest salons in the entire city of Atlanta.

"And my next barbeque, you won't be invited to," she informed him simply.

"Yo, why not?"

"I saw the way you was eyeing Sadie's friend, Malik..."

"Eyein' who?"

Ari sucked her teeth rudely, "Boy don't act dumb. I saw you."

Shit. He was hoping that no one had seen him eye-raping Anika at the barbeque. But he wasn't surprised that of all people who noticed was his Aunt. "No harm in lookin' Auntie."

"Well there's harm, when you're engaged Malik," she responded firmly. "Why'd you keep starin'? I know she's beautiful but damn boy. You couldn't take your eyes off her. You like her or something?"

"She's jus' interestin' to look at," Blaze replied truthfully.

"Your fiancée should be interesting to look at," Ari told him knowingly. "Why didn't she come again?"

"Busy," Blaze mumbled grumpily, remembering the fact that Masika had lied to him about meeting Attorney Coleman. He hadn't brought it up yet because it hadn't affected him like he thought it had.

"She better not be busy for the next one," Ari stated boldly. "She's your fiancée but I hardly know the child. She better make an effort when it comes down to this family or else I ain't coming to no damn wedding."

Blaze exhaled deeply, not even bothering to trying to defend Masika. She was the last thing on his mind right now.

"You hear what I said Malik?" his Auntie queried, wondering why he wasn't responding quickly.

"I hear you Auntie."

After trying his hardest to get Anika out his head and concentrating on spending quality time with his aunt, Blaze figured it was time to head home for a bit before going to do some business with his boys.

Unfortunately, on his way to his red Lambo, Blaze was greeted by an intruder sitting on the hood of his freshly washed and newly painted car.

"Get yo' dirty ass the fuck off my car," he snapped rudely, glaring angrily at her.

"Damn Blaze... Well hello to you too, nigga."

"Are you deaf?" he asked, his frustrations building as he watched her still sitting on his car. "I suggest you get yo' ass off Desiree, before I push you the fuck off. Choose one."

"Baby please, just he-"

He cut her off with a loud chuckle, "Baby? Bitch move."

Messing around with Desiree was a day that he had come to regret but love at the same time. If it wasn't for fucking her, he wouldn't have meet Masika. But at the same time he wished he never met Desiree. She was a pain in the ass that wouldn't go. A rash that wouldn't disappear. No matter how many fucking times he tried getting rid of her, she wouldn't go away!

She stood up, her arms crossed against her pink tank top allowing Blaze to get a top view of her fat titties. He couldn't stand her ass, but she was one attractive female. Clad in a pink tank top, tight blue denim shorts and flip-flops, Desiree moved closer in front of him. His eyes darted up to her cute face, those brown eyes trying to read him, then back down to her slim body.

"Blaze, why you treating me like this? You know how much you mean to me... And I know I mean a lot to you too."

Just as Blaze made a move to head to his car door, Desiree instantly blocked his way.

"Blaze! You needa stop this... You can't ignore me when I know you want me," she cooed gently.

This bitch was really trying him. He was just praying his hardest that he wouldn't have to put his hands on her physically today. He wasn't no woman beater but if she brought out that side of him, it would be her fault.

"I'ma give yo' ass five seconds to get the fuck outta my face, before I make you get the fuck outta my face," Blaze barked, staring down at her, trying to make her feel intimidated.

"This is all because of Masika! You're not supposed to be with her Blaze. I'm the one you met first. I'm the one who really loves you."

5...

"I'm warning you Desiree... If you don't fuckin' go..." Countdowns in his head never ended well. He knew this from experience and messing around with motherfuckers who wasted his time. Time he considered to be precious and very limited.

"You'll do what Blaze?!" She rose her hands up in protest. "Put your hands on me?"

Try me bitch, Blaze mused to himself. *Please just fuckin' try me...* Shooting deadly stares down at her, Blaze decided that the best thing to do would be to keep silent. He didn't give a fuck if this was Masika's sister. She was one thirsty, annoying bitch. And if he had to teach her ass a lesson, then he would.

4...

"I'm not the one you need to put hands on though Blaze! I'm the one who's been holding you down better than anyone else," she continued to rant loudly, still getting up in his personal space.

3...

"I love you Blaze! You're the man for me and I'm the woman for you. Fuck Masika. She's still married to her baby daddy, she don't care about you like I do Blaze. She's irreleva-"

"Baby who?"

Blaze thought he had been hearing shit. But once fully understanding what she had just unintentionally revealed, he had to do a double take. The guilty look suddenly on Desiree's face had him worried. Very worried.

"What'chu mean by that shit Desiree? Baby daddy? Who that? Leek?"

Desiree now decided that this is the time she wanted to keep silent. She even moved out of Blaze's way to let him head back to his car easily.

"Nah, this ain't the time for you to be quiet," he told her firmly, taking a few steps closer to her. "Yo' ass better start speakin' before I make you start speakin' Desiree." With each step he took forward, she took one back. And by the time they had done taking steps, Desiree was pushed up against Blaze's car door, with him right in front of her. He knew she was secretly loving this shit right now but trying to play scared and naive.

"Blaze please..."

"Nah, fuck that!" he began to shout in her face, towering over her short frame. "What the hell did you mean by that shit you just said now?! Masika got a baby with Leek's dumb ass?! Is that what you sayin'?! Answer me!"

"You need to talk to Mas, Blaze," she responded weakly.

"No! I wanna fuckin' talk to yo' stupid as-"

"Alright Blaze!" Desiree suddenly shouted, cutting him off completely. "I'll tell you everything! I promise! Just don't tell her I told you."

Blaze took a deep breath before stepping away from Desiree. He was suddenly fast on his heels, 'round his car so he could get into his driver's seat. He unlocked the car with a touch of his mini button and both his red car doors went flying up in the air. With a stiff nod, he directed Desiree to get in and she quickly obeyed.

Once they were both seated inside his Lambo, with the black tinted windows now disguising them to the public eye, Blaze turned to face Desiree with a blank stare before speaking, "Tell me fuckin' everything and don't you dare leave a single motherfuckin' detail out. Else I'm tellin' Mas about you suckin' my dick last month while I was drunk and she was asleep."

CHAPTER 9 ~ DANCE FOR ME

How fucking dare he?!

Anika couldn't even believe this shit. Not even watching Candi dance was making her happy. Her mood had been completely ruined for the whole night because of him. He was the one that had done this. This was all his fault.

"My wife found out."

"What do you mean she found out?" Anika questioned him rudely.

"She found out," he repeated with a frown. *"And that's why this is happening. I'm so-"*

She suddenly cut him off, *"Fuck your sorry!"* she shouted angrily. *"Jamal stop playing with me... You're joking right?"*

"No... I'm serious. She found out, so we're over."

"We can't be! I love you Jamal!"

"What the hell?" he questioned with frustration written all over his handsome face. *"We were just fucking Anika. This was never love."*

"I love you," Anika pushed, her eyes now becoming watery.

"Stop it Nika," he snapped. *"It's over."*

It didn't matter how many times she pleaded with him, tried to convince him that she was the only woman that he needed, he still fired her.

So here she was, sitting front row at Cheetah Lounge, watching Candi finish up the last few minutes of her shift for the night. Usually Candi was the only one who could cheer her up at a time like this. But now even Candi's talented twerk couldn't turn her frown upside down.

How could he do this? After everything that she had done for him! All the hard work, hours and times she made sure that her pussy was well kept just for him. Anika thought that it had been all a dream. It had to be. Because there was absolutely no way that Jamal Coleman, the man she was sure was going to wife her one day, had fired her today.

It was only now that Anika realized that he never cared about her. He was never going to leave his wife for her. She was just free pussy to him.

Half an hour later, Anika was sitting in Candi's dressing room watching her remove her makeup. Even without her makeup, Candi still looked so beautiful to her. She noticed how her eyes looked much bigger and rounder, but they brought out the beauty deep within her. And the fact that she was now removing her makeup around Anika meant that she was more comfortable around Anika.

"Why you sad baby girl?" Candi stared at Anika's reflection through her mirror. "I saw you sitting out there and you didn't seem yourself boo."

Anika took a soft sigh before deciding to respond, "I got fired today."

"Woah... I'm sorry hun," Candi said softly. "Why though?"

"My boss' wife found out we had been fucking so he had to let me go," Anika stated bitterly, looking down at her purse, ashamed of what Candi would say.

"Woah... So you a freak," Candi commented amusingly, trying to lighten the dull mood. "Well he seems like an idiot for letting you go. Were y'all serious?"

Anika looked back up at Candi's reflection before nodding quickly. "I thought we were... He disagreed."

"What did he say?"

"That we were just fucking, nothing else. He had no feelings whatsoever for me."

"What a fucking jerk," Candi snapped, irritated. "You need to officially take your mind off him Nika baby. He's history now."

"But how am I supposed to forget all that I shared with him Candi? I was falling for him... I developed deep feelings for him and this is how he does me? And to make matters worse I officially have no job."

"Don't worry 'bout him anymore," Candi cajoled her sweetly. "I'm gonna find your pretty ass a new nigga, that's gon' have you speaking a new language every night. And as for your job... Hmm...." Candi paused momentarily, deep in thought before suggesting, "How 'bout you strip?"

"Strip?"

"Yes baby girl. Strip here one night and see if you like it or not," Candi explained with a smile. "And if you do, then cool. You'll be making even greater quicker money than you were making before and only be working nights."

Strip.

Anika had never considered it. She didn't think she had it in her. She didn't even think she could dance on a pole, but there was no harm in trying right? She could do it for a couple nights and use her afternoons to find a new job. It didn't sound like a bad idea...Until the very first night she had decided to strip finally came.

Ass fat, yea I know
You just got cash, blow some mo'
Blow some mo', blow some mo'
The more you spend it, the faster it go
Bad bitches, on the floor, its rainin' hunnids
Throw some mo', throw some mo'
Throw some mo', throw some mo'

"Don't be nervous Anika... Remember what Candi said... Picture your man sitting in the middle of the room, watching you dance for him," Anika whispered to herself, trying to calm her nerves down as she patiently stood behind the shimmer curtains.

Why did she agree to this shit again?

With each loud beat of music, Anika's nerves rose and her heart took a jolt. She was patiently waiting for her que from the music. Candi had requested that she come on stage with her at a certain time, to get the crowd roaring with excitement.

Only Lord knew how petrified she was.

Even though the past few days she had been training with Candi at her house, learning how to rock the stripper pole and shake that booty as best as she could, Anika was terrified. Now dressed in a purple thong and matching thin triangle bikini that hardly did a good job of covering her breasts, Anika was ready to get this over and done with. The theme at Cheetah Lounge tonight was, 'Show your skin, but hide your beauty.' So all the strippers had to wear black masks while performing.

When her music que finally came, Anika fixed her mask on her face, slowly pushed through the shimmer curtains, and sent a quick prayer to the Lord above before walking directly towards the silver pole meant for her.

***

Blaze's mood for the past couple days to everyone expect Kareem and Marquise was *'Don't fucking speak to me, unless I ask you to motherfucker.'*

Everything that Desiree had told him about Masika and Leek had been eating away at him. Constantly making him cranky, angry and wanting to shoot any motherfucker that rubbed him the wrong way. Including Masika and her baby daddy.

Baby daddy.

Blaze couldn't fucking believe it! She had played him for two whole years. Two years she had him thinking that the only reason why she was still married to Leek was because of her laziness, when in reality she had a three-year-old with the nigga.

Even though Desiree could have easily been lying and just trying her hardest to fuck with him, Blaze hadn't bothered to get in contact with Masika and find out the truth yet. He was too blown away, pissed off and frustrated by the entire situation. So he was avoiding her until further notice.

The girl he was engaged to had been playing him for two years by hiding her son away from him. He never got played. He was the one that played bitches! Blaze couldn't seem to get why she would do such a thing in the first place? Why didn't she just tell him from the start of their relationship? Why'd she have to be so fucking sly and sneaky about it too?

He knew that he would have to confront her sooner or later about apparently, not just her three-year-old, but the real reason why she seemed so "lazy" and reluctant to divorce Leek. But all that shit could wait because tonight... tonight Blaze decided to put his mind at ease with a night at his Cheetah Lounge.

He rarely visited. Just because he owned the place didn't mean he had to be there every day. He hired people for that shit instead. But tonight, he wanted to see Candi. He wasn't sure what it was about her that he liked, other than the fact that the mama could dance her ass off. But since Anika liked her, Blaze wanted to like her too.

Anika.

Even with the whole Masika situation, Blaze still couldn't take his mind off that girl. He tried his hardest but it wouldn't work. Especially when he was asleep, showering or smoking a blunt. He pictured her all the time. Either her fucking him or him fucking her, whatever it was - Blaze pictured her doing every freaky thing to him, which resulted in him instantly growing a hard on that he needed to fix ASAP. He needed to see her soon. What they would do, he had no clue yet. *Fuck Masika's feelings.* After spending the night at Cheetah Lounge tonight, he was going to call him cousin and tell her to give him Anika's number.

Ass fat, yea I know

You just got cash, blow some mo'
Blow some mo', blow some mo'
The more you spend it, the faster it go
Bad bitches, on the floor, its rainin' hunnids
Throw some mo', throw some mo'
Throw some mo', throw some mo'

As Rae Sremmurd's 'Throw Sum Mo' sounded through the strip club, all Blaze could do was watch with lust as Candi began to dance, doing all sorts of new tricks on that silver pole and moving her body in ways he hadn't seen her do before. As much as he wanted to join the money throwing crowd that had formed at the edge of the triangle stage, Blaze decided against it. He would just give her an extra tip at the end of her show. He liked watching, more than constantly throwing. He'd rather give his money at the end of a performance. Depending on how much he gave, let a stripper know how well she did.

Blaze continued to watch Candi dance. God damn, she was looking good! She was topless and only wearing heart-shaped sequin pasties with tassels hanging at the end. But she had a black G-string on, covering her pussy as she danced.

Franklins, raining on your body
Raining on your body
Raining on your body
Won't you do what I say
Start rubbin' on your body
Hunnids on your body

It wasn't until the music began to slow down that Blaze realized that another dancer was joining Candi on stage. He sat up straight in his seat, wanting to see who was coming on. Once she walked on stage, a black lace mask covering her face, Blaze was intrigued. He didn't know who she was and he had definitely never seen her dance before. But nonetheless, Blaze watched through hooded eyes as she seductively grinded her body on stage, before wrapping her legs around the silver pole center stage.

The crowd immediately went crazy and started frantically throwing dollar bills on stage, beckoning her to come closer to them. Candi decided to head off, to leave the new sexy dancer on her own. As he watched her move, he couldn't help but begin to compare her to… *Anika.*

They had similar hair, both wavy and long, same skin complexion – light and smooth, and the way that ass moved he was sure he had seen it before. Then when her mask slightly slipped down off her face, Blaze almost fainted.

What the fuck… That ain't… That can't be her!

He suddenly made eye contact with her, watching as she almost froze with fear but quickly shrugged it off like she hadn't seen him and continued to dance. *It's her. What the fuck is she doing here tonight? And on my stage too? Man, I don't believe this shit.*

Blaze wasn't even angry… He was fucking *angry!* He instantly got up out his seat and made his way through the red doors, backstage. *What the fuck was she playing at?!*

Anika ignored Blaze's presence and continued to dance. This wasn't as bad as she thought it would be. It had definitely taken her mind off Jamal and being unemployed. The crowd was loving every single second of her! And looking down on all the dollar bills that were now covering the triangle stage, made her happy. Just as she began grinding towards the silver pole to finish with her last dance move, a hissing noise had caught her attention.

She turned only to see Candi standing near the shimmer curtains, signaling for her to come closer.

"What?" she mouthed quickly.

"You need to get off babe," she whispered loudly.

"Why?" Anika whispered back.

"B' said so."

***

Why you scared for Nika? He ain't your nigga, he can't tell you anything. Matter fact, he should even be thanking you for deciding to dance in his club tonight. See all that mullah you made tonight? Don't worry girl. Just go in, see what the hell he wants and leave.

Anika sighed deeply, knocking twice on his office door before waiting nervously for a response to let her in.

As soon as she was rushed off stage by Candi, before being given a vodka shot, she was sent here. To his office. Like a teenage school girl that had been caught doing bad things by the principal. Like she needed to be punished.

After hearing no response whatsoever, Anika pushed the door open and gently stepped in, hoping that she wasn't about to be shouted at.

"Who the fuck told yo' ass to step in?" His rude question caught her by surprise and from the serious look in his grey eyes, he wasn't playing with her.

"I knocked twice, you didn't an-"

He cut her off, "But who the fuck told you to come in?"

She kept silent and decided that it would be best if she didn't bother saying anything at all. She watched him sitting behind his mahogany desk, legs wide open and his hands laying on his knees as he glared at her. The way he was eye-fucking her half-naked state, up and down, only sent her nerves flying even more.

"I asked yo' ass a question didn't I?"

Again, she kept silent and watched him. Why did she feel like she had done something wrong? All she did was decide to dance tonight.

"So you can't speak now? But yo' ass can twerk half naked on my stage with not a care in the world, right?" he pestered her again, his grey eyes still filled with lust and anger. "Answer the fuckin' question Anika!"

"What?" she queried, her frustrations with him now growing. "I can do whatever the fuck I like. What's it to you?!"

"It's my fuckin' club," he retorted. "No one gave you permission to da-"

"Candi let me," she stated simply, interrupting him.

"Oh, so Candi is the owner of the club now?"

"No, but I figured since she's a strip-"

"Well you dumb as hell for figurin' the wrong shit out then," he barked, getting up out his seat and moving around his desk towards her.

She thought he was going to come closer to her, but instead he began to lean on the edge of his desk, all eyes still on her. But no way was she going to allow this nigga to talk down on her like this!

"No I'm not dumb! I wanted to do something, so I did it. I got fired from Coleman a few days ago, and I needed a job. End of discussion!"

This time it was Blaze's turn to stay silent. He just stayed leaning on his desk and watching her up and down. *Damn... She looks real good though.* Blaze couldn't help but undress her gorgeous body with his eyes. Yes he was angry with her for dancing on his stage but fuck, she looked good! The only reason why he was angry was because he was jealous. Jealous that people were eyeing his beauty in ways that only he wanted to eye her. That bikini was doing a shit job of covering her tits and even as she folded her arms up on her chest, he could still see them trying to be free. Her long legs and ass were out on show too, and Blaze's wandering eyes landed straight in the middle of her thong wanting to be the one to pull it down her legs and get in between her treasure.

"I don't even get why you pulled me off stage! There was no need Blaze, I'm only having fu-"

He instantly cut her off, tired of hearing her rant. "Lose yo' top."

She suddenly looked taken back by his order and asked confused, "Huh?"

"You heard me," he said simply. "Lose yo' top."

"What? No... Why?" She now felt even more exposed and vulnerable to his eyes. Her legs began to take small steps back towards the exit.

Blaze quickly noticed. "Stop movin' ma," he ordered firmly. "I ain't gon' hurt you, I just wan' show you somethin'. You said you wan' dance right? You wan' be a stripper?"

All she could do was stay still in her tracks and nod at him. "Lose yo' top then."

"No... I don't think I sho-"

"I ain't gon' ask you again Miss Assistant," he stated sternly. "Lose the top."

As weird as it seemed, Anika wanted to see what he was trying to prove here. So she slowly turned around so that her back was facing him. Her fingers nervously ran across her sides to her back, where she found the ends of her bikini. As fast as she tried to untie it, she noticed how she was struggling. *Stop being so nervous Anika. Just try and relax.* But even as she tried to persuade herself, it was no use. The strings wouldn't untie. Why'd Candi have to tie them so tight?

"Blaze, I can't..." Her words suddenly trailed off once she felt his presence behind her and his fingers easily untying her bikini top. Before she knew it, the top was dangling off her chest waiting for her to push it up through her head.

Her heart began to pound loudly in her chest as she felt him lift her top off her head, moving her hair out the way so it could slip it over her. She looked ahead as he flung it in front of her. His fresh, warm breath began to tickle the side of her neck as he bent closer to her ear only to whisper, "Turn 'round."

Once she felt his presence no longer as close to her, she turned around only to see him standing a couple steps away. Even though she was completely topless, his eyes weren't on her breasts. They were on her.

"You wan' be a stripper?" he queried with an arched brow, eyes still hard on hers. She nodded slowly, biting her lips shyly. "You need to be comfortable in showin' yo' body," he told her. "Start fuckin' dancin' ma."

"Huh?"

"You heard me," he pushed with a smirk. "Start dancin'."

"There's no music though."

"Did I ask for you to start observin' shit?" he asked, sucking his teeth rudely.

"I can't dance without music Blaze," she explained with a sigh, low-key thinking that this nigga was crazy. How did he expect her to 'start dancing' without music?

"A'ight, you want music? I got'chu."

It didn't take him long to put some music on. He brought out his iPhone, picked a song and placed it on the edge of his desk.

I just wanna show you how much I appreciate you, yes

He nodded at her to do her thing.

"And when I've done this what does this mean?"

"You said you need a job right? Pass this, and it's yours."

Coleman had fired her and blackballed her too. Over the past couple of days, in between training with Candi, she had tried her hardest to find a new job. All she wanted to do was be a new attorney's assistant, but the motherfucker had blackballed her. And she didn't like not having a job. Being a stripper would have to do... Just for a little while though.

Wanna show you how much you got your girl feeling good,
oh, yes
Wanna show you how much, how much you understood, oh,
yes
Wanna show you how much I value what you say,

Anika instantly got right to it. Her hands slowly trailed up her stomach, up her nipples, up her neck then right back down. Her hips began to seductively move to the smooth beat filling her eardrums and her eyes stayed plastered on his grey ones.

As she moved, his eyes began to wander. Those breasts were calling his name to come and squeeze. They were a good size too. Not too big but not too small either. Just the right size. *Fuck... She's even more beautiful without clothes on man.* There was no way that

Blaze was letting her strip at Cheetah Lounge. There was only one person who was going to get to see her half naked from now.

His dick only grew harder and harder with each grind of her hips, and the way those hands were now moving all over her body had him going crazy. He wasn't even touching her, but she still had him feeling so horny and riled up for more. Miss Assistant could dance… No doubt about it. Those innocent eyes of hers were filled with nothing but lust and passion as she continued to dance for him and once she moved closer to him, Blaze pulled her in to him.

Even when she tried to pull away from his grip, he refused to let her go. And she was forced to stare up into those beautiful grey eyes.

Tonight I'm gonna dance for you, oh-oh
Tonight I'm gonna dance for you, oh-oh
Tonight I'm gonna put my body on your body
Boy I like it when you watch me, ah

He spun her around and pushed his crouch against her ass, immediately letting her feel his huge erection poking her behind. She slowly began to tease. Grinding gently on him only making herself more surprised at what she was doing to him. She heard a low groan escape his lips as she continued to sexually grind on him.

"Anika… You know what you doin' to me right now?" His question was a sweet whisper in her ear as she continued to move her ass on his hardness. "You feel that shit?" She slowly nodded, her back still turned facing him.

"I'ma need you to feel it Anika… Grab it."

"What do you mean?"

"Grab this hard dick you caused, right now."

Her heart only began to pound faster and faster, and when she realized her right hand was moving behind her, she felt like her heart was going to burst out her chest.

"Grab it," he firmly pushed and before she knew it, Anika's hand was now in the middle of his pants on his hardness. *Jesus… He's big. No, he's huge!*

"See what the fuck yo' sexy ass done to me?" he asked sexily, a hint of amusement in his voice too. Anika could definitely feel what she had done to him. "Stroke it."

She willingly agreed, gently stroking his large anaconda through his pants and feeling it increase in size by the second. Her horny state had grown from 0 to 100 real quick and before she knew it, Blaze turned her back around to face him and lifted her up by her legs to wrap around his torso.

She wrapped her arms around his neck and once hearing him clear his desk completely by swiping all the objects to the floor, she knew exactly what was going down tonight.

"Blaze…" she gently spoke as he sat her on the edge of his now empty desk, her voice drunk with lust.

"What?" he asked, spreading her legs apart before slowly pulling her thong down her legs, letting it drop to her ankles. Something that he had been wanting to do all night, he was finally doing. *She might regret this later… But I won't.* He wanted to have her. He had been wanting to have her since the very first day that he had laid eyes on her.

"Are we…" Her words were gently cut off once he pressed his lips to hers. Anika swore she felt heaven. His soft lips felt so good against hers and she slowly opened up for him, allowing his tongue to mesh with hers. They refused to stop kissing each other. Their tongues danced, twirled and teased each other, allowing one another to get a sweet taste of their growing desire.

"Lay back," he instructed, pulling away from her lips. "And stop talkin'. Just relax."

She looked up at him as he towered over her and honestly couldn't believe that she was really going to do this. She was really about to give this guy her pussy. A deep breath left her lips before she obeyed him, laying back on his desk.

Blaze got on his knees and lifted each of her thighs to his shoulders. He stared straight at her, noticing how shy she looked. "Stop lookin' so shy, yo' ass wasn't shy when you was rubbing yo' ass and strokin' on my dick," he stated with a sexy smirk. "We both kno' you a bad girl, Anika." Then he dove straight in.

CHAPTER 10 ~ UNDENIABLE CHEMISTRY

"Blaze… Shit, Bla-… Fuck!"

He wasn't one to eat pussy. Shit, he rarely ate Masika's pussy. So the fact that he was so attracted and turned on to eat Anika's pussy had him completely baffled. It looked good too. Freshly shaven and didn't smell. So he figured he might as well try what he had been wanting for so long.

Lord I thank you for this good pussy that I'm happy to receive… His mouth was now buried between her soft lips, sucking on her wet pussy and thrusting his tongue as deep as he could get into her. She started grinding on his face and he pushed his face deeper between her legs, sucking on her some more then thrusting his tongue back into her pussy. His fingers pressed hard into her soft thighs, rubbing the smooth flesh that lay on his shoulders.

"God… Blaze!" *Fuck she tastes good!* He continued to move his mouth over her wet clit, quickly flicking his eager tongue back and forth over it. His eyes suddenly looked up from her pussy to watch the sexual expressions play over her gorgeous face. The faces she was making while he ate her out were enough to make him bust right now.

"Uhh… Blaze, wait… Sto-"

He lifted his mouth off her pussy momentarily to cut her off, "Stop fuckin' running Anika." She had been withering and shaking as he fucked her good with his tongue alone, but now she seemed like she couldn't take it no more.

"Agh! Blaze… please," she moaned loudly.

"Don't let me ask yo' ass again," he threatened with a smirk as he gently stuck a finger inside her tightness. She clearly hadn't had some in a long time. *In. Out. In. Out.* He pushed, enjoying the looks of pleasure fall upon her pretty face. "Stop runnin', you can take it."

He exhaled softly against her pussy before he wrapped his lips and tongue around her clit again, sucking hard and fast on her, trying to get her to cum.

Her whimpers and moans filled the room completely and Blaze was just praying that no one tried to come in. He hadn't locked the door yet.

"Uhh!" she cried out to the ceiling, her thighs shaking as he went deeper between her legs.

"You gon' cum for me?"

"Mmmmmm!" she moaned, holding onto his head, pushing him deeper inside. He gave head better than any nigga she had ever been with. That's for sure!

She whimpered, grinding her hips against his face. He could feel her thighs shaking against his cheeks. She had to be close to her climax. "Uhhhh... Ahh... Oh, Blaze!" The louder she moaned his name, the more she dug her long nails in his back.

Her eyes rolled back under her fluttering lids and her legs shook as he sucked roughly on her clit, grinding his face between her pussy lips as her whole body trembled in his grasp. "Ahhh...Feels so...Uhhh!"

Her body began to jerk and she began rushing her sweet release all over his hungry, waiting mouth. "Mmm..." he groaned, lapping up her sweet cum with his tongue. She looked good and she tasted even better.

Five minutes later, Blaze had locked the door and taken off his shirt and pulled down his pants. Once Anika saw all those muscles and what he was working with, she almost fainted on the spot. *It* was even bigger than she had imagined. Long, thick, hard and wet.

"Where's all that going?" she questioned shyly, watching him tear the magnum sachet between his teeth and quickly strapping up.

He laughed at her before responding, "In yo' pussy. Where else?"

"I don't think it's gonna fit."

He said nothing and went to stand between her thighs, lifting them around his shirtless body. "You still wan' do this?"

His question caught her by surprise but nonetheless, it was too late to turn back now. She nodded and her eyes darted down to his muscular chest. On his left pec he had an angel wing with a few words that she couldn't make out in his dimly lit office. On his right arm, she noticed a large tattoo piece that she would make sure to investigate another time… if there was another time.

He wrapped her legs tighter around him and her hips pushed up against his. She looked up at him lustfully as he slowly filled her tight pussy with his dick.

"Shit, girl…"

"Uhh, Blaze…"

Ecstasy. Ecstasy was the only feeling they could both describe at this moment. And once he started moving and she met him thrust for thrust, the ecstasy only increased.

"Blaze… Too much," she sighed, skimming her fingertips down Blaze's hard back. She knew he wouldn't be able to fit it all in.

"I got'chu baby, just chill," he exhaled in return, gently pecking her soft lips as her fingertips grazed against his muscular back. "Yo' pussy must be made outta gold or somethin'," he groaned, rapidly thrusting his hips forward, burying his dick deeper inside her. He moved his hands to the top of her thighs, pushing her harder onto him. He knew that going faster would only make him cum quicker but fuck it. Her pussy felt amazing!

"Yessss," she hissed in pleasure. "Keep fuckin' me just like that."

"See… I knew yo' ass was a freak," he stated amusingly, continuing to pound into her quicker and quicker. "And a… bad girl too."

She smiled, enjoying the feeling of his dick moving in and out of her. This is what she had been imagining ever since she had laid eyes on him and now that it was finally happening, Anika was gassed.

"I'm… bad for youuu," she moaned gently.

"Only me?"

"Yes," she promised sweetly. "Only you."

And that's how their story began.

CHAPTER 11 ~ ROMANTIC BLAZE

What the hell was he playing at?

Masika's anger was only getting worse and worse with each call that went straight to voicemail. She hadn't seen her man for more than a week now, and he wasn't making a single attempt to get in contact with her. What the hell was going on?

Masika wasn't sure what to think. Was he just busy? Had she done something wrong? Was he in trouble?

All these questions that she needed answers to as soon as possible. He wasn't one to avoid her or not get in contact with her.

Masika needed to see her man.

***

"You did what?!"

"We fucked," Anika responded simply with a shrug. "Exactly what I just said, that's what went down."

"Woah…" A small smile began to creep on Sadie's pink lips. "I don't believe this… You and Blaze?"

"Yes," Anika said with a small nod. "Blaze and I… fucked each other's brains out… On his office desk… Not once… Not twice… But three times."

"Jesus," Sadie stated, clearly surprised. "You are definitely the freak I knew you were. All you needed was a nigga to dick you down, properly."

"So Jamal wasn't dicking me down properly?"

"Hell nah," Sadie replied with a frown. "That nigga had you feening for him all the time, but his dick game didn't even seem all that. But Blaze on the other hand? See, I know my god cousin's a beast when it comes to the sheets."

"And how the hell would you know that?" Anika questioned her best friend suspiciously.

"His girl told me," Sadie explained nonchalantly.

Anika eyes suddenly widened with alarm at her words.

"Ha! You should see your face right now Nika."

Anika sighed softly and relaxed better after realizing that Sadie was lying.

"So she didn't tell you? How'd you know then?"

"Trust me, when you've seen the way females go crazy over him, you'll know too. But then again, you already know," Sadie said with a large happy grin.

"I never even expected it to happen… It just happened."

"You said you stripped at Cheetah Lounge right?" Sadie queried with curious eyes. "Why didn't you tell me? I would have loved to see you doing your thing girl."

"Honestly," Anika began shyly, "I was scared to tell you."

"Why?"

"I didn't want you to judge me and think that I was being stupid."

Sadie suddenly looked at her with a look of disgust. "And why the hell would I think that? You are my best friend, I'm always going to be down for you and supporting you babe, no matter what."

Anika couldn't help but smile at Sadie's kind words. "I know… I should have just told you. But like I said, I was afraid."

"Well cut that afraid shit out," Sadie instructed firmly. "I'm your best friend, I'm not going to judge you. You're my sister."

"I promise I'll tell you stuff more openly from now on," Anika promised softly as she moved closer to her best friend on her black couch and rested her head on her shoulder. "I think Blaze had helped me move on quickly from Jamal."

"Really?"

"Yeah... I mean I hadn't been with anyone but Jamal when we were together," Anika explained. "Now that I've been with Blaze, I feel like it was just lust with Jamal."

"And is it just lust with Blaze?"

"I'm no-"

Anika's words were suddenly cut off by the loud sound of her doorbell ringing. She lifted her head off Sadie's shoulder and sat up straight.

"Expecting anyone?" Sadie questioned.

"No," Anika responded before getting up out her seat. "Let me go see who it is." Slowly Anika made her way towards her door and looked through the peephole, only to feel a sudden flow of shock through her body. *Shit...* Was she dreaming right now?

She quickly stepped away from her door and turned around to face Sadie who was staring straight at her with confusion.

"Who is it?" Sadie asked quietly.

"Blaze," Anika whispered with a small smile.

She didn't know how to describe how she was feeling at this moment in time. She felt surprised, shocked, happy and horny, all in one. And when she eventually plucked up the courage to open the door, there he stood in all his glory.

"Hi," she greeted him shyly, unable to drift her eyes away from his mesmerizing grey ones. How did he know where she lived?

"Hey," he responded warmly.

"How... How'd you find out where I live?"

"I have my ways," he stated confidently before slowly stepping closer to her. Even though she was only in white sweatpants and a black oversized crop top, she still looked so sexy to him. Her hair was up, out her face and she wore very little makeup.

Anika continued to stare at him, observing carefully as he shifted closer to her. Once he pulled her by her waist towards him, she almost felt herself orgasming on the spot. *Chill Nika... You've already had sex with the dude.*

He lightly brushed his lips against hers, still gazing into her pretty brown eyes before responding, "I wan' take you out somewhere."

"Where?"

"It's a surprise," he replied before branding his lips onto hers. The kiss was gentle and sweet, and as his lips continued to work magic on hers, Anika couldn't help but moan between their lips.

He slowly pulled away before adding, "Just go get ready, I'll be in my car out front… And tell Sadie I said hi."

It was then that Anika knew that Sadie was the one who had told him where she lived. When he was gone, Anika shut her door and turned around to see her best friend grinning widely, as she sat on her couch with her legs now crossed.

"You can always count on me to make sure you get some good dick Anika," she commented amusingly with a smirk before adding, "Don't put too much on… I gotta a feeling you won't be needing any clothes by the end of tonight."

***

He was driving really fast, on purpose, just to fuck with her. He liked that she was excited and low-key afraid that his Lambo would be the cause for an early death.

"You good?" he queried amusingly, his foot still heavy on the gas pedal and eyes now on her as he sped down the freeway, anxious to get to their destination.

Was she trying to kill him? That purple dress she was wearing clung onto her slim curvy figure well and only made him more excited for what he had in store for her tonight.

"Yeeaaaah," Anika said shakily with a sigh as she kept her head back against his leather seat. "You always drive this fast?"

"Yup," he replied with a toothy smile, revealing those pearly whites that always seemed to put Anika in a good mood. Even in a simple black tee, black pants and Nike trainers, this man still looked so fucking sexy! All Anika wanted to do was have him all to herself tonight. Over and over and over again.

Even though they had fucked two days ago in his office spontaneously, things seemed chill between them. He had told her that night that he wasn't letting her strip at Cheetah Lounge and she wasn't stripping anywhere else. There wasn't really any awkwardness and hardly any tension between them either. Anika was just eager to know where he was taking her.

When he pulled up to the golden gates and rolled down his tinted window to punch in his code, Anika knew exactly where she was.

His home.

As he pulled up in front of his circle driveway with a large gold lion statue in the middle, Anika's excitement wouldn't stop growing. This man wasn't only handsome but he had money. A lot of it from the looks of things!

While he parked in front of his white steps, Anika stared with awe at the beige mansion that seemed to be getting larger and larger the more she stared at it. His mansion was truly beautiful and she hadn't even been inside yet. The greenery neatly arranged outside, the white tile patio and large golden door, only enticed Anika to head inside and find out more.

She was so preoccupied with staring that she hadn't noticed that Blaze had left the car, jogged round to her side and was now opening the door for her. She liked how polite he was being, even though she had a feeling it wasn't in his nature to be.

Blaze wasn't sure what it was about her, but she made him want to break out from that rough exterior of his and be a gentleman for her. She was a queen. A beautiful one. And he now wanted to be the only one to make her smile.

"So this is where you live?" Anika queried curiously with a happy smile as she stepped out his car and took his waiting hand.

"Yeah," he answered. "Problem?"

"Oh no!" she quickly assured him. "No, it's just so... beautiful."

He chuckled lightly at her before pulling her closer to him and wrapping his arms around her waist. Anika couldn't lie... She loved how he kept doing that to her. She fit into him so perfectly. "Yo' ass hasn't even been inside yet," he explained with a small smirk, gazing into her shy eyes.

"I know. But still... It's perfect."

Just like you, Blaze mused to himself before deciding to steal a quick kiss from her with his hands sliding down her back to her ass cheeks. As he pressed his lips to hers and squeezed tightly on her cheeks, he couldn't help but notice how happy he seemed whenever she let him kiss her. He never kissed Masika this much. Masika hadn't even been to his mansion. The fact that he had bought Anika instead of her, showed how much Anika was becoming more special and important to him.

Ten minutes later, Blaze finally decided to lead Anika into his home. He wanted to surprise her though and keep things interesting still, so he lead her in with her eyes shut and his palms blocking her sight in case she tried to take a peek.

"You can't see nothin', right?"

"No," Anika replied softly, still walking to wherever he was leading her to. She couldn't lie, he had her excited and on her toes. She liked that.

When he finally told her to stop walking, Anika's excitement only heightened and her nerves slowly began to creep up again.

She kept still as she felt Blaze's presence directly behind her and his fresh breath tickling the back of her neck. "Open yo' eyes baby," he cooed sweetly in her ear.

Her eyes gently fluttered open and once she lay eyes on her surprise, she couldn't believe it.

They were in his dining room, which had been darkened with dark blue curtains hanging around. The only light source was from the white candles sitting on the glass table. On the floor there were a trail of red rose petals leading to the table, and on the table lay a red rose with a banquet of food now making Anika's tongue water. From what she could see so far, there was a large bottle of champagne, red wine, yellow rice, meatloaf, green beans, baked mac and cheese, fried chicken, cornbread, yams, pork chops... And even more than she could list out.

"Wow Blaze... You did all this?"

Blaze slowly nodded, watching as she took a few steps forward towards their table to take a seat. He could tell by the surprise and wonder in her voice that she didn't believe him.

"I ain't order none of this shit," he stated proudly. "I made it all for you."

"I can't lie... I'm impressed," she responded truthfully. She didn't think he could cook or even have a romantic bone in his body. "Where'd you learn to cook?"

"My aunt taught me," Blaze said, taking his seat opposite her and watching as she stared at the food with hungry eyes. "You hungry?"

"Starving," she answered with a large smile, now looking at him again with those pretty brown eyes of hers.

"Go 'head," he instructed with a head nod. "Dig in."

Over dinner, Blaze found himself becoming even more fascinated with this beauty. Not only was she smart, beautiful and independent, she could eat! Anika Scott was her full name and she was an only child, losing her parents at a very young age in a plane crash that ended both their lives. One of the main reasons why she was scared of planes. Blaze felt like he could relate to her because he, too, didn't have his parents in his life.

Anika didn't know what it was about this guy, but he was having some type of stronghold on her. The more they talked and got to know each other, the more she was falling for him. He, too, had lost his parents like her. His mother had died from breast cancer and his father had been murdered. He seemed like he had been through a lot but still managed to conquer through it all. Anika also learned how much his Auntie meant to him and how she was the only mother figure he had. She asked him what he did for a living and he said he was a businessman. What type of business he did, he didn't specify and she didn't ask.

But nonetheless, Anika was attracted to this cocky and confident man. And she liked the fact that he was getting so comfortable around her.

"That was delicious," she complimented him sweetly before taking a small sip of her red wine.

"Thanks," he responded gladly. "I'm happy you liked it."

"So when do I get to see a full tour of your gorgeous mansion?"

"Whenever you'd like," he said, his grey eyes hard on her. He couldn't take his damn eyes off her. *She's so beautiful... Why hadn't I met her before?*

"Now would be great," she suggested happily. "Where would be the best place to start?"

"Anywhere you want baby."

She loved it when he called her that. It not only sounded good but it also turned her on. And with the way he was staring at her, her horny state was increasing quickly. Fuck, she wanted him again. Anywhere would do as long as she had him tonight.

"Can I see your bedroom?"

As soon as her question left her mouth, she knew exactly what she had started tonight.

***

He had wrapped her legs around his torso while he led her up the stairs to his bedroom just as she had requested. Their lips refused to leave each other's and the hunger for one another only increased with each step that Blaze took upstairs.

When finally making it to his bedroom, he let her down off him and she immediately began to admire his vast bedroom size that looked fit for a king only. His bare bedroom walls were dark brown, with a lighter carpeted flooring scheme and a large, red king-sized bed sat in the center by the wall, calling Anika's name to enter in.

Anika didn't waste any time. She turned around to face him with a seductive stare, as she slowly began to pull her dress straps off her shoulders and down her body.

All Blaze could do was watch with excitement as she got naked for him. She was so gorgeous. And once left in nothing but her black heels and matching black lace lingerie set, Blaze sauntered closer to her. *I can't wait to remove all that off her… Leaving her in nothing but her heels on.*

The only thing he wanted to do was give her what he knew she wanted right now. He planned to dick her down all night, no doubt. But there was one thing that was eating away at him. Ever since their intense conversation downstairs at dinner, he felt a sudden pour of guilt come over him. The guilt of not telling her what he really did for a living.

"What's wrong?" Anika sensed his sudden apprehensive state. She knew he wasn't one to be shy when it came to sex, so the fact that he hadn't already began to dominate her, had her worried.

"There's somethin' I need to say Anika," Blaze explained quietly, watching her carefully.

She kept silent and decided to wait for him to say what he had to say. Anika figured it wasn't anything serious, but once he took her by the hand and sat her on the edge of his bed in silence, she knew it was serious.

"I wasn't honest with'chu 'bout what I do," he stated guiltily.

"You mean your job?"

He nodded stiffly, before adding, "I'm a businessman, but not the type you think."

"Umm, okay." She sighed softly and kept silent as she waited for him to continue.

"Anika…"

"Yes Blaze?"

"I'm a thug."

CHAPTER 12 ~ DIGGIN' YOU

"Blaze… uh," she moaned passionately. *He's a thug Anika… But you're still here fucking him.*

Anika knew exactly what he did. She knew that he had probably done things in his life that she could never imagine doing herself, but here she was, letting him explore her body and put his mouth in private places that only he could.

Blaze wrapped his thick lips around her hard nipple, sucking it gently with his warm tongue. He lifted her just above his erection, digging his fingers deeper into her round ass. Then he pulled from her nipple with a soft smack, sliding her body all the way down his long shaft.

"Blaze… Fuck!"

"So fuckin' tight girl," he murmured against her throat, slowly lifting her up and down his hard dick.

"That… feels good," Anika gasped, as he thrusted his thick length deeper into her. When they first had sex, he seemed so big but now she was getting used to it. His large fingers dug even deeper into her round ass cheeks, pushing her body all the way down his dick. And when he put his finger in her butt, Anika swore she was going to lose all her sanity.

"Just feels good?" he questioned cockily.

"Feels… really good," she responded with a soft sigh.

Blaze loved that she had such a nice, tight pussy that squeezed around his dick just perfectly. He pecked her lips softly, as she gazed deep into his grey eyes and a sexy smirk formed on his lips.

"You... turnin' a thug... real soft," he groaned bouncing her on his dick between every panted word. She was turning him soft. He was never one to keep kissing during sex and be very intimate with whoever he was fucking. But Anika had that passionate effect on him.

He held on to her even tighter, thrusting himself with force into her wet pussy. Anika loved it when he got aggressive and rough, it felt good. His long arms lifted her body up and down, as he buried his face in her neck, breathed heavily against her skin and used more force to slam his dick into her. He gently kissed her throat, squeezing his biceps around her curvy waist.

Fuck... He's trying to break me. She moaned softly, as he continued to thrust deeper and harder. Her long nails were digging into his back and she had tightened her thighs around him to keep from bouncing too high off him. Anika leaned forward on top of him, pressing her soft breasts into his hard chest.

"Oh Blaze... Fuck me just... just like that," she gently purred, rocking her hips back and forth against his.

"I don't want you callin' me that so much anymore Anika," Blaze ordered firmly, gently pulling her hair back as he continued to fuck her.

"Huh?"

"I want you to call me Malik," he stated as he slowed down his hard thrusts, taking the time to enjoy the sweet tightness of her pussy around his dick. He then started stroking her breasts, and squeezing them tightly in his palms, still fucking her pussy well. "A'ight?"

"Okay... Malik," she responded sweetly before leaning close to his lips and kissing him. He had revealed his real government name to her, meaning that he was starting to trust her even more. She liked that. Her tongue teased its way past his lips, snaking it with his. Then Anika pulled away from his lips, deciding that it was time she took over things.

She suddenly pushed his chest down, resulting in his back to fall to his bed as she stared down at him sexily. He held her gaze, enticingly licking his lips and slid his hands to her hips, squeezing them tight. Blaze was loving the fact that she was taking charge. Usually he dominated in the bedroom, but she seemed eager to take control and he was diggin' it.

"Relax baby," she instructed seductively, her eyes focused on his as she pushed herself up to sit upright on his dick, sinking down as far as she could.

Then she gripped his hands and placed them onto her breasts. Blaze happily reached up to squeeze her warm nipples, teasing them to complete hardness. She arched her back a bit, pushing her breasts out for him to further play with; lowering her hands to brace against his muscular chest as she slowly began to roll her hips, riding his dick.

Blaze bit his lips,, dropping his grey eyes to watch the seductive sight of her curvy hips grinding back and forth, taking his whole length deep into her wet pussy. His hands continued to massage her breasts, rubbing his thumbs over her pointed brown nipples.

"Shit, Anika...fuckin' ride my dick, girl," he groaned deeply, pushing his head back into the mattress of the bed, letting her take complete control.

"Yes baby," Anika moaned, leaning into his warm palms and pressing her fingernails into his shoulders. She grinned once she saw his eyes drift between her thighs, watching as she slid back and forth on his rock hard shaft.

"You like watching me take your big, juicy dick, don't you, Malik?... Every inch of it," she whimpered, lifting herself from his lap until only his hard tip teased her between her wet entrance, and bringing herself down hard onto him again.

He nodded, groaning deeply, "You take my dick so fuckin' good, baby." Blaze wasn't one to talk about how well a girl fucked him. Shit, no girl really fucked him. He fucked her. So to have Anika to be the one to do something different had him feeling on cloud nine. *She's so different... I'm loving it.*

"Damn... You keep fuckin' me like that with that bomb ass pussy and I swear to God, I'm gon' have to wife yo' sexy ass," Blaze loudly groaned, gripping her hard nipples tighter between his fingers. Yeah, things between them was going really fast. But so what? He liked her and knew she liked him too.

The more she fucked him, the more he felt like he was going to burst. She bounced on his dick and the sexy sounds of their skin slapping filled the room.

Anika brought her hands up from his body, entangling her fingers with his over her breasts as she continued to bounce eagerly on his thick length.

"Ohh fuck yes, Malik!" she moaned loudly, and Blaze knew she was getting closer and closer to her orgasm. "Oh, it feels so fucking gooood... Shit..."

"You trust me Anika?" Blaze suddenly asked as she continued to ride him, her lids were growing heavy over her brown eyes but she could still see the serious look on his face as he questioned her.

She nodded, still riding him as his walls clenched tightly around his dick.

"I wan' hear you say it baby," he requested firmly.

"I trust you Malik."

***

"Did you know?"

"Well... I had a feeling, but I never asked hun," Sadie explained truthfully. "Are you afraid?"

"No... I don't think I am," Anika said. "He's... interesting."

"Well of course he's interesting, when you've been fucking him for the past two days."

"Sadie!"

"What?" Sadie asked amusingly. "Girl you know it's true. You can't get enough of him and he can't get enough of you. You're getting to know each other better and before you know it, you'll be in a serious relationship."

"I'm not sure about all that…"

"What's there not to be sure about?" Sadie queried with confusion. "You like him. He likes you."

"Masika," Anika whispered sadly. "I don't know what the status of their relationship is. They were engaged when I first met them."

"Fuck Masika," Sadie snapped. "… But if it's really bothering you then you need to ask him about it. You're not living that side chick life again, uh-uh. Jamal was already enough trouble."

Anika couldn't help but laugh lightly at her best friend, "I swear… You're something else Sadie."

"And that's why you will forever love me."

Fifteen minutes after speaking to her best friend, Anika left Blaze's on-suite bathroom and walked out only to see him still in bed. He looked cute while he slept and Anika wanted nothing more than to continue to cuddle with him for the whole day. *Guess I wore him out yesterday… and this morning,* Anika mused happily.

She quickly made her way inside his bed, pulling the covers off his body so she could move next to him and lay by his side. Then she brought the covers back over them both and snuggled up in the warmth.

Anika figured he was still sleeping, but once she felt his hands pulling her closer to him and his arms wrapping around her waist, she knew he was awake.

"Who told yo' sexy ass to leave me in bed alone?" he asked boldly, his grey eyes suddenly flying open and staring at her with happiness and lust.

"I had to call Sadie," Anika responded shyly, with a small smile. "She kept texting me to know if I was okay."

"Nah, she kept textin' to know if I dicked you down good last night."

"And she already knows that I fucked you good these past two days," Anika replied smartly.

Blaze chuckled lightly at her, pulling her closer to him. "Oh…I see you got jokes, huh?"

"Hmmm… A bit," she stated with a large smirk before branding her lips onto Blaze's. She loved kissing him; it made her feel good knowing that they were being intimate all the time. It made her feel like he belonged to her, even though she knew he actually didn't.

"Malik, we-" Anika's words were cut off in-between the kiss and Blaze refused to take his lips off hers. Even when she tried pulling away, he still kept kissing her. "Mali-… Ma… Malik please hold on," Anika stated desperately, with a firm hand now on his hard chest, stopping him from trying to kiss her again.

"What?" he queried with a groan, still eager to join his lips back on hers.

"Malik… We need to have a talk," she began boldly. "About us."

"What 'bout us?"

"Us," Anika repeated with a small sigh, looking down at his angel wing tattoo that had a memory poem dedicated to his mom, with the pink breast cancer symbol at the end of the wing. Her fingers gently trailed across it as she waited patiently for Blaze to speak.

"Well, you know I like you," Blaze admitted, lifting her chin up so she was forced to stare at him again. "And I know you like me too."

"I do, but you're engaged Malik," she reminded him. "To a woman you know much better than me."

"To a woman I thought I knew," he corrected her. "But all that don't matter because I'm with the woman who I want to get to know better and start somethin' with."

"But what about Mas-"

Before Anika could even get her next sentence out, Blaze's doorbell sounded through the mansion, cutting her off.

"You expecting someone?"

"Nah," Blaze shook his head no. "And I ain't down to see no one but you right now."

"But you sho-"

The doorbell sounded again, cutting Anika off.

"Go answer the door Malik," Anika cajoled him sweetly. "I'll still be here."

"I don't wan' answer though," he retorted. "Whoever at the door can fuckin' go."

"But what if they don't g-" Another ring cut her off.

"You know what?" Anika asked with a sudden look of determination. "I'll go answer the door."

"A'ight baby," Blaze responded simply. "Gimme a kiss before you go."

Anika quickly obeyed and kissed Blaze sweetly, before rolling out his bed and grabbing his nearby red robe.

She was running down his golden steps, while putting on his robe and eager to tell whoever was at the door to go away. Once finally reaching the door, Anika swung it open only to look ahead with shock because of who was now standing in front of her.

"Blaz-... Wait... What?! Why the fuck are you here bitch?!" she asked rudely with fury growing in her eyes, as she watched Anika in nothing but a red robe. All Anika could do was stare at her with shock and slight fear.

Masika Brooks.

CHAPTER 13 ~ WATCH YOURSELF

"Are you fucking deaf bitch?!" Masika continued to question her. "What the fuc-"

"Firstly, watch your mouth," Anika snapped at her, cutting her off. "Secondly, I'm here because Blaze wants me here."

Anika knew she was playing with fire here. Here stood Blaze's fiancée who looked like she was ready to beat her ass. But Anika wasn't scared. If Masika decided to lift a single finger on her, she would be ready to attack.

"What the... are you sure you're at the right house little girl?"

"Little girl?" Anika asked her with a raised brow. "Bitch, you better watch yourself."

"Or what? What can you do hoe?!" Masika shouted, stepping into Anika's face. "You know I'll wipe your boney ass across the floor!"

"Boney ass? Girl, your 'man' was feeling up on my ass all last night and this morning," Anika revealed with a devilish smile.

Masika had heard enough. Seeing Coleman's ex-assistant standing in front of her, in her man's mansion and wearing his robe had her infuriated. And knowing that they had fucked each other only made things worse. *So this what this nigga had been doing instead of answering my fucking calls?!*

"Bitch, I'ma fuck you up," Masika threatened before charging straight for Anika. But as soon as she aimed to take a hit at her, Anika was immediately pulled back out the way.

"Baby, chill... Just go upstairs for a minute," said a deep baritone voice that instantly began melting Masika's anger away.

Masika thought he was talking to her, but once stepping inside his mansion and noticing Blaze and that bitch holding hands, she realized he wasn't. Her heart felt like it was being slowly crushed into little tiny pieces.

"But Malik, I want to s-"

"Uh-uh," he cut her off sternly. "Wait for me upstairs."

"Malik?! Who the fuck is Malik?!" Masika exclaimed furiously. She thought she was dreaming. This had to be a dream, right? There was no way that this shit was happening. But even with her shouts, Blaze and Anika ignored her protests.

Once Anika was out the front room, Blaze's attention was now on Masika, who looked like she wanted to burst into tears. He didn't care though. She was going to have to find out sooner or later, right? Better now than never.

"Blaze... What's... going on? Why is she here? Who is Malik? Why have you been... ignoring me?" she questioned him, getting emotional. Tears were now filling her eyes.

"Stop actin' so dumb Masika," Blaze berated her. "What's goin' on here is that I know yo' ass has a son with Leek! And you've been lyin' to me for two years now!"

Masika froze with fear as she stared into Blaze's grey eyes. The only thing she could think right now was...

How the hell am I going to convince him that I have no son with Leek? I can't fucking lose him!

***

Anika sighed softly, continuing to listen to their never ending battle downstairs.

"Who told you I had a son?! Was it that bitch upstairs?"

"Don't you dare talk 'bout Anika like that in front of me," he threatened her. "She hardly knows yo' ass to say that you have a son."

"So who the hell told you a bunch of lies Blaze?"

"So you don't have a son?"

"No!"

"Masika, there's no point in lyin' to me..."

"I'm not Malik!"

"Chill, it's Blaze."

"So that hoe upstairs can call you by your government name but I can't?! How come you never told me your real name Blaze?! How come I've never spent the night here?"

"Do you have a son with Leek or not?"

"I don't! The only son I want to have is with you! No one else."

"So you tellin' me you don't have a son with Leek?"

"No Blaze..."

"Are you absolutely sure?"

"Yes."

"So if I was to ask Leek before I kill his ass, he would say the same?"

Masika suddenly kept silent.

"You kno' what? I think it's time you left."

"No Blaze! Please ju-"

"Get the fuck out Masika and on yo' way out leave the ring."

"No! Blaze, please don't do thi-"

"Don't make me tell yo' ass again Masika. Fuckin' go and make sure you leave yo' ring on the way out."

"I'm not going anywhere Blaze!" Masika suddenly protested angrily. "I don't know what the fuck you think you playin' at, but we're in engaged to be married because we love each other. That hoe upstairs must have done some voodoo on your ass! You don't just stop wanting your fiancée Malik!"

"What the hell I tell you 'bout calling me that?" Blaze questioned her in a snappy, angry tone. "Don't make me tell yo' ass again. It's Blaze."

"I AIN'T FUCKING GOING ANYWHERE... MALIK!"

Anika saw this as the perfect time to intervene on their conversation. She was tired of hearing Masika's shouts and protests, as if it was getting her anywhere. It really wasn't. Blaze wasn't trying to listen to anything she had to say. So Anika was going to personally see to it that she left.

"He already told you to leave," Anika retorted as she walked down Blaze's golden middle house stairs. "So why the fuck are you still here?"

"Bitch, who the hell was talkin' to your stupid ass?!" Masika shouted loudly, trying to get to Anika but Blaze quickly blocked her path. "I'm at my man's crib, I can do whatever the fuck I like!"

"Well your *man* is asking you to leave," Anika snapped at her. "Seems like you need some extra assistance when it comes to walking out someone's door."

"Oh, so you wanna assist me now?" Masika questioned her, taunting her. "Alright then, bring that ass here girl and come *assist* me. I promise you you'll be the one needing assistance ho-"

"That's enough Masika," Blaze exclaimed, cutting her off completely. "I'm tired of hearin' yo' voice right now." And just like that Blaze had grabbed her by her shoulder and was now pushing her out his door.

"So this is how you gon' treat me Blaze?! After eve-" *Slam!* "Blaze! Let me in right fuckin' now!" After slamming the door in her face and leaving her outside, Blaze ignored her loud, rapid knocks and turned to face Anika, who was still standing on the steps with a pissed off expression on her pretty face.

"Thought I told yo' ass to stay upstairs?"

Blaze expected a quick, smart reply from her but instead came a tired sigh followed by a rude suck of her teeth.

"Who the hell you suckin' your teeth at like that Anika?" Blaze asked her sternly, not liking the way she was suddenly behaving towards him.

"You want me Malik? Well, I'm not going to be another man's side chick. You better sort *her* out or else... I'm gone," she announced with a frown before turning on her heels back upstairs, leaving Blaze to stare at her with a blank expression as she left him with his troubled thoughts.

Masika's gon' be a problem... He could already tell.

CHAPTER 14 ~ VOODOO SHIT

"Who the hell could have told him? You don't think it's Leek, do you?"

"Des, I don't fuckin' know. All I know is that when I find out who did this shit..." Masika said with an angry sigh. "I'm going to kill them with my bare hands, I swear."

Desiree kept silent at her threatening words, not wanting to add fuel to her sister's fire. She was the one that had revealed to Blaze everything. And as happy as she was, she was shook! If Masika found out that it was her who told Blaze about Tarique, she knew her days on earth would be very limited.

"Don't even get me started on that bitch I found at his mansion," Masika snapped with disgust.

Desiree's silence was suddenly shortened. "What bitch?"

"My attorney's assistant. Well, ex-assistant. When I went to see him a few days ago and asked where she was, he said he had to let her go. Silly old me didn't even realize that the first time I brought Blaze to his office, this hoe was checking out my man!"

Desiree's jealousy quickly began to build. "How do you think she got Blaze to talk to her?"

"I don't fucking know!" Masika shouted loudly. "She must have done some type of voodoo shit or something. I swear... when I see that bitch again it's over for her. I'm going to kill her."

Desiree didn't know what to think. Blaze suddenly has a new chick? It didn't really make any sense to her on why he was automatically with someone else after claiming Masika all these years and putting a ring on her finger. But this new chick didn't matter to Desiree. She was just happy that if Blaze was fucking somebody new, Masika was no longer on his mind. And that would mean that when it came to making him hers, she would have no problems.

***

"That dumb nigga Leek thinks he's getting away with this shit. He must not fully know who the fuckin' Knight Nation are," Marquise commented with a smirk. "We got eyes everywhere lookin' for this fool. He's bound to be found soon."

"We need to find him sooner than later. He's been sellin' our shit on the streets. Our shit that he stole! We can't let him get away with this," Kareem responded, his voice filled with nothing but determination and slight anger.

As eager as he was to get to Leek and deal with him for what he had done, Blaze had other things on his mind. Things that didn't involve Leek right about now, but involved his fiancée and a new woman in his life that he knew he was quickly falling for.

Ever since his date night with Anika, which turned into two days of just getting to know each other better and pure fucking, Blaze couldn't be happier. But when Masika decided to show her face on his doorstep, Blaze was no longer in his happy mood. Anika didn't seem to be happy either. She had been ignoring his calls for the past week and when he texted her, she claimed she was "too busy finding a job." After all, her being fired from Coleman left her jobless for the time being.

When she had revealed to him why she was fired, he couldn't believe it. What it looked like to Blaze was that because Coleman and Anika fucked, he couldn't face the true reality every day looking at his assistant, knowing they were more than just work colleagues. But all that shit didn't matter to Blaze. What mattered was getting to know Anika even more and being the one to look after her. He wanted to make sure that from now on, she didn't lift a single finger. He wanted to be the one to look after her, care for her and give her everything she needed and more. He wanted to be the only person who she needed to depend on. He wanted to be her man.

"Boys... don't sweat," Blaze assured his boys. "Like Marq jus' said, we've got eyes lookin' for this fool everywhere. And when we find him... he's a dead man."

Kareem and Marquise nodded at him in agreement, before focusing on the numerous medium sized packages lined up in front of them. "How much you think this shit is B'?"

"Probably over four hunnid pounds... Connect said he wanted us to shift double the weight, this month," Blaze responded to Kareem, as he lifted one of the brown covered parcels up and slowly teared off the paper to examine the contents. Blaze stared down at the large weight of white powder in his hands. "It's gon' be a lot of work, but we gon' get it done."

"I'll call some of the guys in a bit to come start pickin' this shit up," Kareem announced.

"Sounds like a plan," Marq replied with a grin before adding, "Speakin' of some shit... Yo B', what's up with you and Masika?"

Blaze rolled his eyes in annoyance before deciding to speak. "Apparently this bitch has a son with Leek."

"What?!"

"Apparently?" Marquise questioned suspiciously. "So you ain't sure?"

"I'm not a hundred percent sure but I have a feelin' it's true."

"So are you still with her?" Kareem queried curiously.

"Not really. I mean, after findin' out that shit and realizing that she's been keepin' this away for two years kinda made me think, fuck her. So I've been vibin' with this new chick."

"Oh word?" Kareem asked.

"Yeah... I ain't sure what it is about her, but she's really different. Different than Masika and any other chick I've been with put together. Not only is she sexy as fuck, but she's intelligent, sassy and independent. If all goes well, I think I might have to wife her ass."

"Woah, you can't wife her without us meetin' her first B'," Marq declared seriously. "She gotta get our stamp of approval before anythin' else. We yo' brothers, and we know what's best for you. Right Reem?"

"Yeah, yeah," he said in agreement. "We don't wan' another Masika to pop up."

Blaze couldn't help but chuckle at his boys lightly before commenting, "Trust me, she's no Masika. But if yo' silly asses really wan' meet her, then cool. I'll set up somethin' soon."

An hour later after leaving his boys at their main warehouse, Blaze was now on his way to his aunt's salon. It was 7:30pm and Blaze was praying that she was still around fixing someone's weave or braiding someone's hair.

He hadn't seen her in ages and he wanted her advice on his current situation. Masika, his fiancée was someone who he wasn't sure he wanted to be with anymore, but Anika was someone that he wanted to be with. His feelings for Masika hadn't completely died down though. The only thing he was unsure about when it came to Anika was whether or not her being with him was a good idea.

She knew what he did for a living, but he wasn't sure that her knowing was a good thing. They hadn't really discussed it that much. Only briefly spoken about him being a thug and then fucked the living day lights out of each other.

Blaze needed his Auntie Ari's advice more now than ever.

When finally arriving, Blaze noticed how dim the salon lights were inside and once entering, he only spotted his Aunt's assistant sitting by the main reception booth. Deeper inside the salon were a few hairdressers, fixing up a few last minute clients.

"Hey Blaze," she greeted him happily, with a large smile. Bitches always seemed to be extra happy when he came around here. "How may I help you handsome?"

He gave her a sexy smile before asking for his aunt's whereabouts. Unfortunately, she had gone home early, leaving Blaze to wonder if he would be willing to make the drive out to her house, which was a two-hour drive to Lakewood heights.

Fuck it, he needed to see her. She was the only woman who gave him the best advice. She would help him decide what to do about Masika and Anika. Just as he turned around to head out, he was stopped by the sudden call of his name.

"Blaze! Wait up!"

Blaze sighed with frustration at the fact that this bitch was here. Why is that whenever he came to his aunt's salon, she seemed to be here too? He dismissed hearing her voice and turned quick on his heels out the exit and towards his car.

However, just as he made it out and was now entering his car, she came running, still calling his name and trying to grab his attention. "Blaze! Wait!"

"What Desiree?!" he shouted at her, no longer being able to hide his anger away from her.

"Blaze... Hi," she said quietly, still quickly walking towards him as he stood at the foot of his car door.

"What do you want?"

"I need to speak to you Blaze," she explained gently.

"Yo' ass speakin' right now, ain't you?" he questioned rudely, not down to listen to whatever bullshit she had to say to him right now.

"I told you the truth about Masika and this is how you do me?" she asked with an arched brow with surprise. "I could have kept shit away from you and let her string you along like her little puppet."

"Oh, so you wan' a fuckin' cookie bitch? A medal perhaps?"

"No Blaze!" she exclaimed, now getting emotional with him. "I love you Blaze and I know you love me too."

Not this shit again. Blaze decided that it would be best if he just left. Clearly Desiree was crazy, something that he realized from the very first day after fucking her.

His butterfly car doors rose up into the air and he got in, before pulling them back down again and shutting his door loudly, blocking out Desiree's protests.

All he could see as he sat in his car, was her mouth moving and her eyes filling with water. *This bitch needs to get a life*, he thought. Blaze didn't have time to be dealing with her right now. He needed to get to his auntie's ASAP. She was the only one who would tell him the right thing to do about Masika and Anika.

As his engine began to roar and his foot on the gas pedal, Blaze was ready to leave. However, there was one thing now stopping him.

She was purposely blocking his way by standing at the front of his car, and all Blaze could do was stare at her in disdain at her current plan for his attention.

"I'm not going anywhere," she mouthed with nothing but seriousness and determination fixed upon her face.

Staring at her with his arms crossed as she stood outside, made him suddenly realize how good she was looking. Wearing only a tight leather jacket and black tight skirt, revealed those legs and curves of hers and because of how big her breasts were, the leather jacket could hardly close over her chest.

Call it whatever you like, but Blaze's dick was slowly standing up at attention the more he stared at her staring at him. When was the last time he had gotten some?

There was only one way that she was going to be happy and shut up and the more Blaze watched her, he knew he was just going to have to give it to her...

~ *Thirty Minutes Later* ~

"This what the fuck you wan' bitch?! This how you wan' me to fuck you?!"

"Yassssss daddy," Desiree moaned loudly, "This how I want alllll that big dick."

Blaze knew it was going to happen sooner or later. Better it happen now and never again.

One hand was wrapped around her throat, the other wrapped on her bouncing tits that kept jiggling with each thrust of his dick inside her. All that could be heard was his groans, her moans, their skin slapping together and the sound of his dick moving in and out of her wet pussy.

"Fuck! Yo' pussy so fuckin' wet…"

"Wet only for you daddy."

Her voodoo on him all of a sudden was strong. A few days ago, if someone had told him that he was going to fuck Desiree, his fiancée's sister, he would have straight up punched them in the face and told them they were a damn liar. But now, shit was popping between them. She had definitely changed up her sex game too. He didn't remember her liking niggas choking her out while they fucked her from the back. She was definitely one freaky bitch…A freaky bitch that Blaze knew he couldn't mess around with ever again.

***

Staring up into his hazel eyes was nice and all, but it didn't matter how fine he was, with that tall 6'1" height, cute dimples, straight white teeth, plump kissable lips, smooth milk chocolate skin, sexy muscular physique, low fade hair cut with a freshly trimmed goatee that lined up perfectly against his lips - this nigga was staring to piss Masika off. All she needed was a simple, truthful answer. She knew he knew where her man was at. "I asked you a question didn't I? Where the fuck is Blaze at?"

"Chill… And I just answered you Masika, he's not around," Marquise answered her sternly, still blocking her way as she tried to get past him. "Go home ma', I'm sure he'll call you soon."

"He's too busy fuckin' that hoe to call me or even pick up his damn phone! Marq, just please tell me where he's at," she begged desperately.

"Just go home Masika… I'll tell him to call you when I see him. But I can guarantee you he's not here. It's jus' me. Why the fuck would you even come here alone Masika? You know how dangerous it is." Masika knew that coming to Blaze's main warehouse wasn't a good idea, but she was willing to do anything to see her man. She needed to see him.

"I don't care!" she exclaimed loudly. "I need to see him. I need to talk to him… He thinks I have a son-"

"And you don't?" Marq asked her suspiciously.

"No! Whoever told him that shit is just trying to ruin what we have. Marq please believe me…" She looked at him sincerely, hoping he believed her.

"You sure?"

Time to be the great actress you know you are girl. Masika nodded gently and small tears began to flow out her eyes. "Please believe me, Marq." If she could get Marquise, Blaze's best friend on her side, then getting Blaze to believe her would be a no brainer.

"Don't cry ma'," he whispered softly, using his fingers to gently wipe away her tears before opening his arms out to her. "I believe you."

All Masika could do was smile with happiness and slowly went into his warm embrace, letting him comfort her.

I'm going to deceive this fine nigga and get my man back… Just watch me.

CHAPTER 15 ~ FUCK YOU TALKIN' TO?

"She won't let you in Blaze, just go home," Sadie advised honestly.

"Nah, she has to let me in," Blaze responded firmly. "I don't care how long I have to knock on her damn door."

"But she told me last night that she doesn't wanna see you," Sadie said quietly.

"Well she's a damn liar then," Blaze snapped. "Must have forgotten how good I dicked her down all those nights ago!" he shouted as he began knocking loudly on Anika's white apartment door. "Open the fuckin' door Anika!"

"Blaze... Chill! You don't want all her neighbors to start coming out, do you?" Sadie questioned him. "Let me call her and speak to her, then I'll call you back. Alright?"

Blaze sighed deeply, before deciding that his god cousin's plan would be best. "A'ight, do that. And tell her if she don't come to the door in five minutes, I'm breakin' in."

"Don't you dare Blaze," Sadie warned seriously. "Just let me speak to her and find out where her head's at."

Once their conversation was over, Blaze tightly held his phone as he rested against her door, hoping that she would come and open it as soon as she was off the phone with Sadie. All he wanted to do was talk. It was clear to him that she was still trying to avoid him and was probably pissed with him because of the whole Masika situation.

He hadn't had the chance to speak to his aunt yet, but he had a strong idea of what he wanted to do with Anika. And it certainly didn't involve Masika. All he wanted was a chance from her to let him show her that he wanted to try things out with her. He wanted to lay everything out on the table and see where things went between them. But all his wants would be completely pointless if she didn't let him in.

Ten minutes later, Blaze heard a click then a latch unlock, which quickly made him move off her door and turn around. Her door slowly opened and instead of welcoming him in, she just left the door open.

Blaze strolled in, closing her door behind him before focusing his attention on her. It was only 11.30am, so to see her in her seductive black silk robe on a Sunday morning was no surprise. She looked beautiful. From the last time he had seen her, her hair was in its usual wavy state, but today it was completely different.

Anika was rocking box braids which she had packed up into a perfectly neat bun, showcasing those gorgeous facial features of hers. Blaze continued to stare at her up and down, admiring the way that silk robe fitted so wonderfully around her curvy figure. He badly wanted to be the one to untie her robe and touch every single pa-

"What do you want Blaze?"

Her question immediately cut off his lustful thoughts and he was forced to snap back to the reality; she was pissed with him.

Anika didn't like what he was doing to her. She didn't like it one bit. Clad in denim black jeans, a white, short-sleeved Ralph Lauren polo with black Nike Air Forces, Anika found herself drooling over how sexy he looked standing by her door, watching her. Those muscular arms... Those sexy eyes...That tall irresistible height... That large print in the middle of his pants... *Fuck, this man was fine!* It didn't help that he was looking good and that she was angry with him, because all she wanted to do was jump on him, but also shout at him too.

"I came to see you," he responded simply, his hands now buried deep in his pockets and his eyes fixed on hers.

"Why?"

"'Cause yo' ass been avoidin' me and I don't like that shit Anika," he retorted.

"Well you know exactly why I've been avoiding you Malik."

Oh shit... Government name. Shit's getting serious, Blaze mused worriedly.

"I'm sorry 'bout Masika poppin' up like that," he apologized sincerely. "I didn't even know she was gon' do that shit. And I'ma make sure it won't ever happen again."

Anika kept silent and just looked up at him, wondering if he had anything else to say. But Blaze just kept silent too, observing her carefully.

"You got anything else you wanna say?" she queried curiously, crossing her arms tighter across her chest.

Blaze quickly shook his head no. "Nothing at all?" she asked again, a look of fury starting to form on her pretty face.

"Nah," he responded sheepishly.

"Okay then, shut my door on your way out."

"Huh?"

"You heard me," she snapped. "Shut my door on your wa-"

He suddenly cut across her, "I ain't goin' anywhere Anika."

"Yes you are," she stated sternly. "You said you don't have anything else to say, then you can fucking go."

"And who the fuck do you think you cursin' at right now Anika?" Blaze wasn't liking this newly found attitude of hers at all.

"AT you Malik!" she exclaimed, pointing at him rudely. "I'm cursing at fucking you!"

"I don't know who the fuck you talkin' to right now, 'cause it certainly ain't me Anika!" He shouted, taking small steps forward away from her door. With each step he took forward, Anika slowly stepped back. "I came here to talk to yo' rude ass, but it seems like you got me fucked up."

"You're the one that's not being clear about what you want Malik!"

"Oh… I'm the one that's not bein' clear?" he questioned her sarcastically. "But look who the one that wants me to fuckin' go!"

"You're engaged! To someone else that isn't me. So what the hell do you want from me Malik?"

"You know what I wan' Anika. I told you this shit already when I had you in my crib," he said, becoming frustrated with her.

"Well it seems like you're just playing games with me," she declared.

"How the fuck am I playin' games Anika?! I told yo' ass already I want to start something with you," he fumed, moving to stand in front of her.

She looked up at him, becoming slightly intimated by the way he was towering over her and glaring down with those grey eyes. "But you're still engaged with Masika! I'm not going to be your side chi-"

"But who am I fuckin', you or Masika?"

She kept silent for a while before answering with a shrug. "You could be fucking some other chick."

"But I ain't!" he shouted, knowing deep down he was lying. But fucking Desiree was a mistake that wasn't going to happen again. He would make sure of it. "I'm only fuckin' you, because I only want to fuck you!"

"But what about Mas-"

He suddenly interrupted her. "I'm endin' shit with her, so don't worry 'bout her."

"But yo-"

"Anika, don't let me have to tell yo' ass again. I'm done with her, and anyone else. I want you, a'ight? You the only one gettin' this dick from now on, a'ight?"

Anika slowly nodded, biting her lips sexily at him. All his shouting and him going off on her had low-key turned her on. And now she wanted him.

"So stop fuckin' worryin' about shit that don't matter!" he concluded loudly before walking straight past her and heading straight for her bedroom.

Anika stayed still in her place, smiling to herself as she thought of how she was loving Blaze's dominant and cocky side towards her. She already knew that he wasn't one to mess with, but she liked messing with him.

"Get yo' sexy ass in here!" he shouted from her bedroom and she quickly obeyed, running blissfully to her bedroom. "Yes daaaddy," she sweetly sang.

Once inside, she noticed him sitting on the edge of her lilac king-sized bed and watching her seductively with those grey eyes that she loved so much.

"Get naked," he ordered firmly, still watching her carefully. He couldn't wait to get in between those tender thighs of hers and give her a good dicking down that would assure his new commitment to her.

Anika slowly untied her robe straps, pulled it off her body, letting it fall straight to the ground. She smiled sexily as Blaze's eyes widened with lust and she sauntered closer to him, until she was sitting on his lap with her legs folded against his thighs.

His hands went straight to her ass cheeks and gently rubbed on her firm flesh, before moving his head closer to the side of her neck.

"Malik..." Anika gently moaned his name as he got right to work. Rubbing on her ass and kissing her neck, was rapidly driving her crazy and she wanted nothing more than to feel his thick, long length buried inside her.

Things only got more heated between them once Anika started rubbing her naked pussy on Blaze's rock hard erection, teasing him to complete hardness.

"Fuck... Anika, you know what you doin' to me right now," Blaze gently groaned in her ear, moving his big hands up her body and using his thumbs to play with her nipples.

"I want you so bad," Anika whispered, her voice drunk with lust and sex.

"Hmm... How bad you wan' me baby?"

"So fucking bad," Anika said with a soft sigh, still grinding on his hard erection. "I want to... feel your big dick inside me... Fucking me... Making me cum all day."

Shit... She's talkin' real dirty. Blaze felt his whole body heat up with excitement at her words. *Got a nigga blushin' and shit.* The way she had said them sounded so hot to him.

"You know you a bad girl right?" He questioned her sexually, rubbing his hands down her back again.

"I'm bad for you," she responded blissfully.

"Only me?" he asked, gently lifting her chin up so he could stare directly into her pretty eyes while she spoke.

"Yes," she promised sweetly. "Only you Malik." She then branded her lips to his and kissed him passionately.

Anika knew that she was quickly falling for this guy the more they spent time together. The sex was bomb, their time spent with each other was becoming better and better, and she was getting to know a side of him that she knew he didn't show so easily. Yes, she was falling for him badly. It was uncontrollable and growing every day. She was just praying that he didn't break her heart...

~ *1 Month Later* ~

"Yo' fat ass is always hungry," Blaze commented with a light chuckle as he continued speeding down the freeway.

"Hey!" Anika exclaimed with a smirk. "A girl's gotta eat."

"So what my girl lookin' to eat today?" he asked, his eyes looking momentarily away from the road to stare at her pretty face.

Anika smiled happily, trying to conceal her delight at Blaze calling her *'His girl'*. One month of being with him and she still couldn't help but continually get gassed when he called her that. Like she belonged to him.

"Wherever my man's planning to take me," she responded calmly.

"It's a surprise baby," he cooed sweetly. "Jus' relax and enjoy the ride."

"Hmm... Okay," Anika said with a gentle sigh. "What you feeling like doing after?"

"I'm cool with doin' whatever you wanna do as long as I'm doin' it wit' yo' pretty ass."

Anika couldn't help but blush and smile at his words. This was one of the main reasons she loved being with him. He made her smile with his sweet words. And he wasn't one to be sweet by nature. She was the one bringing the sweetness out of him.

"You're so sweet Blaze," Anika informed him.

"Sweet?" Blaze questioned her with an arched brow, his eyes still plastered on the road ahead. "I ain't never been called that shit."

"Well... I guess I'm calling you it now," she responded with a shrug. "You mad?"

"Nah baby," he assured her quickly. "You think I'm sweet? Then I guess I am for you."

"Yup!"

Blaze lightly chuckled at her before announcing, "I swear yo' ass turnin' a thug real so-"

Ring, Ring, Ring!

Blaze eyes suddenly diverted from the road ahead to his car screen monitor in the center of his controls. It indicated an incoming call from Kareem. Even though he was taking a day off to spend some time with his girl, business was business. Blaze contemplated whether or not to pick up but his thoughts quickly cut off when Anika stated calmly with a hand to his thigh, "Pick up Malik... It's cool, I don't mind."

And this is one of the things he loved about her. She was always so understanding and considerate.

Anika watched silently as Blaze pressed the answer call option and listened in on his conversation with his friend Kareem, who she had heard so much about but yet to meet. Same with Marquise. Blaze had told her a lot about them and how much they meant in his life. So meeting them would definitely be around the corner. The only thing that Anika didn't know was how soon that corner was quickly coming.

Kareem's deep baritone sounded through the car speakers and Anika's ears jolted up, focused on their conversation.

"Yo nigga," he greeted Blaze simply.

"'Sup man?"

"Where you at?"

Blaze turned briefly to stare at Anika before focusing back on the road. "I'm with bae... I told you guys yesterday I'm busy today. That's why I took a day off."

Bae. He had never called her that before. And hearing it out his mouth sounded so good to Anika.

"Well, you gon' need to come in now lover boy."

"What the... Why?" Blaze queried rudely.

"Got an emergency, a 308."

Blaze's grey eyes widened with surprise and his hands tightened around the steering wheel.

"Got'cha. Usual spot, yeah?"

"Bet," Kareem concluded before ending the call.

Anika wasn't sure what exactly a '308' was but she knew from the way Blaze reacted, it wasn't something good.

"Malik, what's going on?" she asked worriedly, watching him as he continued speeding.

"Nothin' baby," he stated in a quiet but firm voice. "I jus' quickly gotta do somethin'. I won't take long."

Ten minutes later, Blaze had pulled up to an abandoned warehouse, given Anika a passionate kiss and promised her again that he wouldn't be long.

"Don't leave the car Anika. Not at all. You need somethin', call my cell. But I ain't gon' take that long so you probably won't even need to do all that." He gave her another passionate kiss, before leaving his Lambo and Anika.

Anika watched through hooded eyes as he entered the old building, leaving her all alone. She honestly wasn't sure what on earth was going on, and quite frankly she was more hungry than confused. But she was still concerned. All she hoped that Blaze wasn't in trouble. She definitely didn't want that. *He's a thug Anika, he's always in trouble... Matter fact, he's the trouble. He probably has a lot of enemies too girl. Enemies that are going to become your enemies if you keep fucking with him.*

For the past few days, Anika had been having some doubts. Dating Blaze was great. Beyond amazing. The conversations were good, their chemistry was out of this world and the sex? BOMB.COM. However, there were a few things bothering Anika, and no matter how hard she tried to shake them off, they would still build.

Masika... His dangerous profession... His loyalty... All these doubts were just building in her head the more she tried to push them away. Especially when she was by herself. And she didn't like it one bit. Anika needed something to take them completely off her mind.

And that's exactly what happened ten minutes later, when Anika noticed one silver Range Rover aggressively pulling up next to Blaze's tinted car.

She couldn't see who was in the car, because like Blaze's windows, the car's windows were tinted. But once four men covered with black ski masks, two holding machetes and two holding firearms, exited the vehicle, Anika's panic instantly flew through the roof.

Her heart began to pound rapidly in her chest as she watched them, looking at her. She thought for a minute that they could see her but she suddenly remembered that Blaze's windows were tinted. *Thank God,* she sighed softly, observing carefully as they stopped looking at the car and made their way towards the same building Blaze had entered, ten minutes ago.

What if Blaze was now in trouble? Those men didn't look like they were here for a meeting. They looked like they were out for blood.

He told you not to leave the car Anika. He said call his cell, so just do that before you start jumping to conclusions. So that's exactly what she did. She quickly rambled through her silver purse only to bring out her gold iPhone and immediately dialling Blaze's number.

Unfortunately for her, he didn't pick up. All Anika could hear was the ringing dial of the phone, before it headed to voicemail. She didn't bother leaving a voicemail. Instead, she tried calling again. "Malik, pick up your damn phone!" She called five times. Still no fucking answer!

Relax Anika… He's fine. He wouldn't just come here by himself with no help inside, right? Then a sudden chill ran down Anika's spine when she realized that other than Blaze's car and the four masked men's car, no other car was out here, in this foreign place.

You've got to go in, Anika sighed deeply before beginning her search of Blaze's car. She needed to get what she needed before leaving this car and risking her life for this man. This man that she had now fallen for.

When the silver pistol appeared in a secret compartment behind Blaze's driver's seat, a small ounce of relief poured through Anika's system. But then she realized that she might have to use it and the relief immediately went flying out her.

You said you were going to be down for him, Anika. Take this as one of the ways to be down for him by making sure he's okay. Anika took a deep breath, before holding the pistol tightly in her right hand and leaving Blaze's Lamborghini.

With each step she took on the grey concrete towards the chipped black painted door, Anika felt like she was going to faint. Her palms felt sweaty, her knees felt weak and she was sure that her hands were shaking.

Get yourself together Anika. Your man could be in danger and you're out here being a pussy. Quickly, she followed her own advice and decided to woman up and stand up for her man. Regardless of if he was in trouble or not, she still needed to be sure that he was cool.

Anika took her last deep sigh before pushing the door open and gently stepping inside with her pistol right by her side.

"Yo Blaze... she's here!"

"Damn, she got yo' gun too!"

What she then witnessed made her want to kill them all.

CHAPTER 16 ~ HIS TRAP QUEEN

"Baby, you still mad at me?"

Anika said nothing and just kept quiet as she watched him through angry eyes. Even his question was pissing her off further.

How could she not still be mad at him? After what he and her boys had put her through a couple of hours ago, mad was an understatement.

What she witnessed made her want to kill them all.

They were all sitting around a wooden table, Blaze at the center, one of his boys at the right side and another on the left. The right side one had the biggest grin on his face, as Anika stared at him angrily. All they seemed to be doing was playing a card game, until Anika walked in.

"Yo... You got a loyal, brave trap queen over here B'," the one on the right said. Blaze said nothing and just smiled happily as he got up out his seat.

"Baby, yo-"

"What the fuck's going on Blaze?!" she questioned him furiously, watching him walk towards her. "You left me alone out there! And then I see four guys, with machetes and guns enter in here!"

"Anika, let m-"

"What kind of sick game are you playing with me Malik?! I almost risk my life to check up on you and here you are playing fucking cards with your boys!" she exclaimed, interrupting him, fired up and infuriated with him.

Blaze paused momentarily before asking, "Yo' ass done shoutin' now?"

"Yes," she mumbled sulkily.

"I didn't know about what just happened until I came in here. Kareem," Blaze said as he pointed to his boy on the right, "...was the one who planned this shit with Marquise, behind my back."

Anika looked at the boys, still annoyed. They were still grinning at her and watching her carefully. Both of them were handsome. Very handsome indeed.

Woah Anika, chill. You already got a man.

"They said they wanted to meet you, but they ain't say when exactly. So imagine my surprise when I turn up here, thinking we have an emergency but they planned this shit to test you, to see if you were really down for me. And now I can see that you are baby," Blaze concluded lovingly.

"Yeah Anika, you the realest and baddest trap queen Blaze ever had," Kareem commented.

"And you ain't no punk," Marquise stated boldly with a smirk. "I like that shit."

Anika didn't really give two flying fucks about some silly test. She was still pissed. She couldn't believe that Blaze would put her in that position. He said he didn't even think she was gonna leave the car, after he told her not to. He was going to play one card game with his boys and come right back out to her. All that shit didn't matter to her though. What mattered was the fact that she was made to believe that Blaze was in danger when he really wasn't.

"Baby, I already apologized," Blaze commented gently, moving across his bed to where she lay. "And yo' ass still playin' games."

I don't give a flying fuck if you begged nigga, Anika mused privately, but she didn't utter a single word to him. She just rolled her eyes at him and looked away, trying her hardest not to become turned on by his attractive, shirtless body, but it was so damn hard!

"So you just gon' keep ignorin' me?" he queried seriously. "Anika."

Her head was turned away from him, her focus clearly not on him, starting to frustrate him. He didn't like the way she was acting towards something so small, something that didn't matter anymore. The moment had passed, so why couldn't she just let it go? He didn't want her angry with him for the rest of the day. He had a gift for her.

"Anika, look at me," he ordered. She didn't bother obeying him though. "Anika, don't make me have to tell yo' ass again," he fumed, his eyes staring hard at the side of her head.

Still she didn't obey. Knowing that she was playing with serious fire here, Anika shut her eyes and sighed softly. A nice little nap would do her justice right now.

However, just as her body began to adjust to the idea of taking a nap, Anika felt her legs being tugged and pulled across the bed. Her eyes quickly shot wide open only to stare right into the mesmerizing grey eyes of Mr. Malik King.

"Malik! Leave me al-"

"Who was the one who told yo' ass not to get a new job?" he questioned, cutting her off. His hands were now holding her legs by his sides and not letting her go from his sight.

"Malik, let me g-"

"Who was the one that told yo' ass not to get a new job Anika?"

"You were," she responded sulkily.

"Why?"

"You said you wanted to be the one to provide for me."

"And what did yo' silly ass say?" he asked with a cheeky smirk.

Anika shot him a cold glare before answering, "I don't need a man to take care of me. I can take care of myself."

"And what I say?"

"That you're my man... And," Anika paused momentarily before chuckling lightly. "You don't care if Bey's gassed me up thinkin' girls run the world. I'm your woman and whatever is yours, is mine. You'll always be there for me and protect me."

"Exactly," Blaze responded. "I was never gon' let anythin' bad happen to you today. I would never let that happen Anika. So dead that angry shit right now. My dick is hard and in need of yo' pussy ASAP. So stop fuckin' playing ma', we got unfinished business to handle right now."

"Malik," Anika sighed with a small smile. "I know you wouldn't have let anything bad happen to me but I didn't like that your boys were testing me I'm the first place. What if I failed? Then what?"

"But you ain't fail bae," Blaze replied happily, gently stroking her ankles. "You passed and now they like you much better than before."

"I don't know Blaze..."

"Stop stressin' Anika," he cajoled her. "They like you and even if they didn't I wouldn't care, because I like you and that's all that matters. A'ight?"

"Okay baby," Anika said with a simple nod before lifting her back off his bed and leaning close to his lips.

"Someone's dick still hard?" she questioned in a sexy whisper across his thick lips.

"Uh-huh," Blaze said, licking his lips at her. "And someone knows she needs to handle daddy's dick."

"And she will," Anika promised as she moved her hand to Blaze's large bulge in the middle of his boxers.

"But first," Blaze began, lifting her hand away from his dick, "I got somethin' I need to show you."

Five minutes later, Anika was blindfolded and made to stand in a certain place in Blaze's bedroom. She could tell they hadn't left his bedroom because the flooring was still the same texture against her feet.

"Malik... Can I take off my blindfold yet?"

"Hold on." She could hear his footsteps moving across the room but she wasn't sure what on earth he was doing.

When it was time to remove her silk blindfold, Anika was greeted to a dark pink door which Blaze instructed her to open. When she opened it, the look on her face had Blaze happy and full of love at the fact that she was excited and liked her gift.

Anika couldn't believe it. The further she walked in and began to admire the nude painted walls, the oak floor and the various designer clothes, shoes and accessories organized neatly for her, she wanted to faint.

"Malik... Oh my gosh! All this... For me?"

He had designed her own closet space filled with all the designer brands a female desired. Chanel, Gucci, Prada, Christian Louboutin, Nike... She couldn't even name them all! There were too many. The rows of clothing and shoes seemed to be endless and the more she began to admire, the more she began to want to cry. He had done this all for her. Nobody else. All for her. Anika slowly turned to face him. He was standing in the doorway, his arms folded across his muscular chest and the largest smile upon his handsome face.

"You like it baby?" he asked with an arched brow, already knowing her answer.

Anika didn't bother saying any words. She figured it was best to show him just how much she loved it. She slowly walked up to him and once standing in front of him, she looked up and branded her soft lips to his.

The kiss was heaven on earth for Blaze. One thing he loved doing, was kissing his lady, Anika Scott. Not only was she a great kisser, she knew how to enchant him from the very first swirl of her tongue against his. He loved the way she kissed, tasted and danced their mouths together.

Both her arms went around his neck and his arms went around her slim curvy waist, pulling her closer to him. His hands found their way to her ass cheeks and firmly began to squeeze while moving her away from her new closet and back towards his bed.

Their lips momentarily pulled off each other's, so Blaze could talk to her.

"You like it?"

"I love it Malik, thank you so much," she sweetly thanked him.

"You gon' show me how much you love it?"

Anika nodded sexily, before moving from in front of Blaze to behind him. She roughly pushed him, making him fall back onto his red, king-sized bed, causing it to gently bounce.

He looked up at her, with a wild look of excitement now in his grey eyes. He could tell she was about to dominate him, bringing out the freaky side of hers that he had grown to love so much. His freaky Anika.

"Take your boxers off," she ordered firmly. "Now."

Once they were off, Anika got right to work. Her hands quickly wrapped around Blaze's large dick and her tongue began sucking on his hard tip. One hand was pumping up and down at the bottom of his base, while the other gently stroked his muscular chest.

"Nika... Shit... Reina ... me gusta esa mierda." *(Queen... I like that shit.)*

Anika knew that whenever she brought the Spanish out Mr. Malik King during sex, she was bringing out an emotion that only she could. An emotion that Blaze knew all the other girls he had been with in the past had failed to do properly, including Masika. It was just the amazing way she was making him feel and her ability to do it so passionately and easily.

When her slick mouth began rapidly moving up and down his hard dick, Blaze's groans couldn't stop. And when she started sucking not just on his dick but his balls as well, with her freaky mouth spitting on him and licking all the nasty mess she had made, Blaze felt tiny tears sliding down his cheeks.

"Fuck! Uhh... Uhh... Agh! Anika... You bad, freaky girl."

Her head game was out of this world! And with the way she was pleasuring him, he knew just how much she loved her gift.

***

"So the last time you were in contact with him was a month ago?" Desiree questioned her sister curiously, before taking a small sip of her lemonade.

"Yeah," Masika stated helplessly with a sigh. "He changed his number up on me and whenever I try to find him, he's not around. It's like he's avoiding me."

Masika was getting sick and tired of Blaze's "breakup." As far as she was concerned, her fiancé was Blaze and she was going to get married to him before the end of the year. This whole charade he was playing needed to stop. Masika was sick and tired of it.

"And you said you spoke to his boy, Marquise? Did he promise to speak to Blaze for you?"

Desiree didn't know why she was bothering to ask her sister questions she didn't really care about finding the answers to. Blaze didn't belong to Masika anymore, Desiree knew that for sure. Her only real mission was getting Blaze to be her man and being the rightful woman wearing his ring, not Masika. Desiree was honestly tired. Tired of pretending to care how her sister felt and what she wanted, when all Desiree felt and wanted was Blaze - her man.

"I think I need to get Marquise to help set up a meeting with Blaze and I," Masika announced confidently. "Blaze must be trippin' if he thinks I'm letting him go! It's all that bitch's fault."

"Do you know if they're still fucking with each other?" Desiree queried quietly, secretly masked with envy and jealousy. She didn't like this new chick either. The fact that she was trying to take her future man was an issue for her, and Desiree knew she would need to get rid of her one way or another.

"I'm not sure... But I'll get some information from Marquise. Hopefully he tells me," Masika said with a small shrug. "I just can't sit back and watch this hoe take my man! He belongs to me and I'm not letting him go."

You and me both sister, Desiree mused privately. *You and me both.*

***

"I hope she ain't get too angry with you 'bout what we planned."

"Nah," Blaze paused momentarily to take a deep inhale of the blunt, sitting in between his fingers. "I put her ass in check already and made it up to her." Blaze smiled at the memory of him and Anika yesterday, chilling, talking and making love.

What they were doing, it wasn't just fucking anymore. Blaze had a feeling from the very start that it wasn't just fucking, but he went along with it anyway. Now though, things were clear and obvious for him. He was falling for her, badly and quickly.

"She seems loyal as fuck," Kareem commented blissfully, before taking a deep pull from his blunt too. "You love her?"

"I don't kno'," Blaze responded truthfully. "We've been together for a month now and I ain't gon' a single day without her sleepin' by my side."

"Yo, she livin' with'chu now too?"

Blaze nodded simply before replying happily, "I even got her, her own closet space set up and everythin'. With a couple Gucci, Chanel, Prada... The whole shit."

"Damn!" Kareem exclaimed with widened eyes. "Pussy must be bomb to have you this whipped nigga. Masika ain't even have you like this."

Blaze deeply sighed, "I kno'. I don't really know what she's doing to me but I really like her. I'm even thinkin' about the future and shit... stuff you kno' I don't do when it comes to females. But Anika's different. I'm really diggin' her personality too. Like, I see that chick as my wife, poppin' out my seeds and shit," Blaze revealed truthfully.

"Oh word? What 'bout Masika?"

"Masika... I don't kno'," Blaze stated calmly. "I had feelings for her but it ain't as much as how I feel for Anika."

"So why don't you just cut her off?"

"That's the thing I ain't done yet. I ain't even talked to her since last month. I changed my number on her and I've just been kickin' it with Anika."

"Wait, so you haven't ended shit with Masika?"

Blaze nodded stiffly before answering, "Nah... I haven't."

"And how Anika feel about this?"

"She don't even kno'. I told her I'm done with Masika, but in reality that bitch still has the ring and probably believes we're still together," Blaze stated frustratingly.

"You need to get that shit sorted out now man," Kareem warned him lightly. "Before it comes back to bite you in the butt. And you kno' Anika ain't gon' be happy knowin' you ain't cut Masika off completely."

"I kno', I kno'... I'll sort it out soon. I just haven't been down in seeing Masika 'cause she's too fucking clingy and demanding. Then she'll start cursin' out Anika makin' me want to choke her the fuck out," Blaze retorted.

Kareem let out a hearty laugh before commenting, "Seems like you and Marquise are the only niggas with lady problems. See me over here? I'm straight."

Blaze grinned at Kareem, knowing deep down Kareem wanted someone too. He had always classified himself as a *'I only fuck pussy, not claim it'* man, but Blaze knew his friend all too well to know that he wanted someone who he could settle down with in the future.

"Speakin' of Marquise, where he at?" Blaze queried curiously, wanting to know the whereabouts of Marq.

"You know that new chick he's been messing with?"

"Yeah, what 'bout her?"

"Turns out she's married," Kareem stated sheepishly.

"What?!" Blaze couldn't believe this shit. He had known that Marquise had found a new chick who he was really feeling and hoping to spend the rest of his life with. So to find out she was married was a complete shock to Blaze.

"Yup," Kareem reiterated with a simple nod. "Married with kids and shit."

"So where is he?"

"I'm not sure. I texted him but he didn't reply. I'm guessing he just wants to be left alone."

"Damn... The shit must really be hurtin' him too, because he said that he was falling in love with her," Blaze revealed gently.

"I kno'," Kareem stated in agreement. "You boys and yo' female problems... That's why being single is so much easier."

"I kno', but you don't wanna be single for the rest of your life Reem," Blaze advised seriously. "It ain't fun forever."

Kareem sighed softly before shrugging reluctantly. "I ain't really lookin' for no female to tie down to right now. But if she happens to come my way very soon, then I guess I'ma be straight. But for now, pussy is pussy. I'ma just keep doing what I want and enjoyin' this single life while I still can. It is what it is man."

***

The smell of freshly fried plantains filled the house as soon as he stepped in. His mouth began to water and his tongue was already beginning to imagine the succulent, sweet taste of the foods he could smell.

"Baby... Where you at?" Blaze called her out to her loudly, slowly walking through his mansion as he continued to follow the delicious smell he could now almost taste.

Finally making it to his kitchen, Blaze was greeted by a seductive goddess, in nothing but a pink silk robe, hands on the marble kitchen countertop, smiling happily at him.

"You're just in time," Anika greeted him warmly. "I cooked you a little something."

Anika had definitely not just cooked Blaze, a little something. As his eyes began to wander, his stomach began to growl with even more hunger and anticipation for some food inside him already. On the kitchen counter in front of her, there were various dishes and bowls filled with the plentiful foods that Anika had cooked for him.

It wasn't even Thanksgiving but with the amount of food she had prepared just for him, Blaze knew that Thanksgiving had come early.

Two hours later, after having a feast together, Blaze and Anika found themselves cuddling and chilling on his black loveseat, with a Netflix show playing on the plasma in front of them. With his arms wrapped around her and her body leaning against his, the both of them felt so in love by being in each other's arms.

"You enjoy the meal I made for you?" Anika questioned him shyly.

"Course I did," he responded. "You definitely need to do that shit more often."

"More often Malik?" Anika's left brow rose up in surprise and a small smirk grew on her lips.

"Yeah, more often bae," he pushed. "Like every single day."

"Uh-uh!" Anika protested sternly. "That meal took ages Blaze, and I'm still drained from standing in the kitchen all day. Besides, you can cook right? Cook you something to eat tomorrow."

"But I want my lady cookin' for me," Blaze whispered gently, moving his soft lips to the side of her neck. "She's the only one who can throw it down in the kitchen."

"Uh-uh, I know what you're trying to do Malik, and it ain't gonna wor-. Mmm, Malik," Anika gently moaned at the feel of Blaze's lips kissing on her sensitive neck.

"Say you'll cook for me baby," Blaze cajoled her sweetly between his seductive kisses.

"Mmm... Uh-uh...Malik you can cook for yourself."

"I kno'. But I want you cookin' for me tomorrow, in nothing but yo' panties on."

Anika couldn't help but fall in love with his neck kisses. And when she felt that warm tongue of his swirling on her skin, she knew she was officially a goner. "Mmm Malik… Nothing but my panties on?"

"Absolutely nothing," he whispered sexily into her ear.

"How about we ditch the panties and I cook you breakfast in nothing but my Louboutins?" she asked sexily. "Actually, I don't even really need to cook anything. You got everything you need to eat right between my thighs. All you gotta do is get on your knees and eat this pussy."

"Damn Nika, you bad girl," Blaze stated amusingly. Her confidence was turning him on, he couldn't lie about that.

"I'm bad for you," she replied lustfully.

"Only me?" he asked, lifting her chin up so she was forced to stare up into those mesmerizing grey eyes of his that she adored so much.

"Only you Malik."

CHAPTER 17 ~ MISSING YOU

"Malik, I haven't seen you in like forever boy."

"I kno' Auntie," Blaze stated with a deep sigh. "You said you got another barbeque comin' up?"

"Uh-huh," Auntie Ari confirmed. "You comin'?"

"You ain't gotta tell me twice," Blaze said with a light chuckle. "You already know I'll be there."

"Yeah, stealin' all my food," Auntie Ari answered.

"I even got a surprise for you Aunt-"

"Seriously?"

"Yeah," he reassured her. "Just wait and see."

"Any hints?" she questioned him sheepishly.

"Nah, you just gotta wait and see."

"Alright boy, just don't go giving your aunt a heart attack," she advised carefully. "Ain't nobody got time for that."

Blaze was sure that his auntie was going to love the surprise he had for her. She was the one who had first noticed the interest he had in Anika, so for her to find out that they were together would be a surprise for her. Good surprise, Blaze hoped. He just really wanted his aunt's blessing on their relationship so he could start taking things further, to a greater level.

Anika was one bad chick who Blaze could seriously see spending the rest of his life with. She was now that special to him and the way he felt about her was absolutely no joke. He wouldn't mind taking her down the aisle or letting her have his seed in the next coming years. He was really digging her.

Blaze quickly brought out his smartphone and headed straight to his messages to see if his baby had replied to his last text.

She had.

Anika: "I miss you too."

The last time he had seen her was two days ago and being away from her was now bringing withdrawal symptoms for Blaze. They were apart because Blaze had business to take care of. He couldn't be wait to have her back in his arms though, and smelling into that seductive scent of hers was sure to drive him crazy with love.

Malik: "Just come see me now."

Anika: "No Malik. You're busy and I'm currently job searching."

Malik: "Wait... Job searching?"

Anika: "Yes."

Malik: "After I told yo' ass not to, Anika what the hell?"

Anika: "I'm joking Malik! I'm not job searching."

Malik: "You sure?"

Anika: "Yup! I'm going out with Sadie in a few hours."

Malik: "Can I come with, baby?"

Anika: "Nope! Girls only."

Malik: "I miss you though."

Anika: "I know, I miss you too... But I haven't had the chance to see Sadie in like forever."

Malik: "When am I gon' see you next tho? Tonight?"

Anika: "I'm not sure... We're going out for drinks then probably to the strip."

Anika: "Not Cheetah Lounge though..."

Malik: "So yo' ass trying to avoid me or somethin'?"

Anika: "No baby. I wanted us to try some place new... Don't take it personal. I promise we'll see each other soon though."

Malik: "We definitely have to see each other before my aunt's barbeque in two weeks."

Anika: "Oooo, she's having another one?"

Malik: "Yeah."

Anika: "Cool! Guess I'll see you then."

Malik: "Stop playin' Nika…"

Anika: "Whose playin'? I'll see you then."

Malik: "Now I see you tryin' to get in trouble."

Anika: "Trouble?"

Malik: "Yes trouble."

Anika: "With who?"

Malik: "You already kno' who."

Anika: "Nah.. I don't… Enlighten me :)"

Malik: "Next time I see yo' ass you getting' a spankin'."

Anika: "You can't do shit xxx"

Malik: "Is that so?"

Anika: "Yup!"

Anika grinned down at the bright screen of her iPhone, knowing that she was playing with fire here but she didn't really care. She liked playing with Malik. It kept things interesting and exciting between them.

Instead of getting a quick reply from him, Anika's phone went quiet. She waited for a few minutes before feeling the sudden vibration from her iPhone, telling her that an incoming call was coming through. Seeing his name appear on her screen made her face light up with happiness and excitement.

"Hello?"

"Oh, so you think you funny right?" His sexy deep baritone immediately sent shivers down her spine, making her heat up with lust all for him.

"Hey Blaze," she greeted him gently, trying to remain as calm and she possibly could. Just by hearing his deep voice was driving her crazy with passion for him.

"Answer my question," he said firmly. "You think you funny?"

"Maybe," Anika's eyes gently shut as her head rested comfortably against her bed headboard. *Does he not know what he does to me? Even just listening to his voice is making me want him even more.*

"Well we'll see how funny yo' ass is when I have you bent over wit' yo' ass stickin' out so I can give you a good spankin'.'"

"Damn Blaze," Anika stated with a soft sigh. "A spankin' only?"

"A spankin' not good enough for you? You wan' some more?" he questioned her curiously, getting the idea that things over the phone between him and her were going to get very interesting. It had been a long time since Blaze had had some phone sex. The last time he had done it was a few months ago, when Masika left town for a few days. A nigga was horny as hell, and the only way he could think of pleasing himself was listening to Masika's voice while he beat his dick.

"Yes," she responded shyly. "I want some more."

"Stop actin' so shy Nika," he instructed her softly. "If you wan' do this, I'ma need you to tell me exactly what you want. A'ight baby?"

Anika took a deep exhale and her eyes gently fluttering open before lifting herself off her headboard before replying, "Okay Malik." All of a sudden she was craving phone sex with her man. Maybe it was because she hadn't gotten some from him in two days now, but she wanted him now more than ever before. "I want you so bad right now baby…"

"How bad you want me Anika?" He queried seductively.

"So bad," she whispered sexily. "I've been thinking about you, that big dick… And how I want you to put it in me."

"Oh really? Well… I've been thinkin' 'bout you too baby, that tight pussy... And how bad I want you ridin' me all night."

Listening to him talk about how he wanted them to have sex, had drove Anika to new limits. She was now slowly unzipping her jeans and pushing them down her thighs. "Blaze… Keep going."

Hearing her gentle voice and knowing that she was probably touching herself because of him, was driving him on edge. He had now pushed his hands down his pants, under his boxers and already began to stroke his rock hard erection.

"You gettin' naked for me baby?" he asked.

"Yeah... You?"

"Nah... I can't right now, but I'm beatin' my dick thinkin' about you. I can't wait to see you and be inside you beautiful."

"I can't wait to see you too... I can't stop touching myself without thinking about you Malik," Anika responded.

"What part of yo' body you touchin' bae?"

"Whatever part you want me to touch Malik."

Shit. Blaze's strokes were beginning to get faster and he didn't want them to. He wanted things to go nice and slow but the pleasure was too intense for him to slow down now.

"Stroke those juicy breasts for me." Anika immediately obeyed, feeling the erotic pleasure within her, suddenly overwhelm her, unable to conceal her moans.

"I'm stroking baby," she replied with a sweet whisper. Her hands gently rubbed on both her breasts, while her iPhone rested in between her shoulder and ear.

Hearing her moans through the phone was driving Blaze even more insane than before. She sounded so hot! All he wanted was to be with her in person so they could skip the foreplay and get right to business, but this would have to do for now. "I now make a trail of kisses on your breasts, down to yo' stomach and instantly meet yo' sweet pussy..." Blaze could hear Anika's breathing go heavy. "I want you to stroke yourself for me baby, just the way I would."

Again, Anika listened to Blaze and once her hands were in her panties, she started rubbing gently, feeling into her wet arousal. "Oh baby..."

"How many fingers can you fit inside babe?" Blaze couldn't stop himself even if he tried. Hearing Anika on the phone masturbating was driving him beyond insane. His strokes began to get faster than before. Up, down, he quickly stroked.

"Ummm, two," she whispered shyly.

"Put two fingers inside your pussy, and tell me how it feels."

Anika obeyed, putting her two fingers inside her and slowly pulling them back out. "It feels good Malik," she gently moaned. "So damn good," she continued to finger herself. In, out, feeling the wild sensations running through her body.

"Fuck baby. You sound so fuckin' hot. I'm so hard right now," Blaze groaned, continuing to stroke himself. "All I wan' right now is you, completely naked and on my dick."

"Uhh... me too. I can't wait, I need you deep inside me Malik, right now... Shit." Anika knew she was on the edge now.

"Baby don't cum yet... hold on," Blaze groaned, hearing his woman's moans get louder.

"Uhh! Malik..."

Malik's strokes suddenly became faster and faster. He knew he was going to reach his high any minute now.

"Baaaby... I'm gonna..."

"Go ahead baby, cum for me," he ordered her.

They both climaxed at the same time, hearing each other enter their euphoric high together, moaning and groaning. They could hear their heavy breathing on the line and they stayed silent for a while.

"Nika... That was amazing."

She giggled innocently, before replying, "I'm glad you enjoyed it babe. I enjoyed it too."

"That's good. I can't wait to see you again... You got a nigga feenin' for you every day he ain't wit'chu."

Anika couldn't help but smile at his comment before answering. "I can't wait to be with you again."

**

"So?"

"So what, Sadie?"

"So how's things going with you and my cousin?" Sadie queried with a smirk. "I know he's been dicking you down good enough, but how are things between you guys? Like the relationship side."

Anika smirked at her best friend before speaking, "Things are going good... Great even. Remember when I told you he told me not to get a job?"

"Yeah and you disagreed, but he insisted," Sadie said.

"Well... he's been looking after me and I hardly even live in my own apartment now."

"Wait, so you guys are like living together?"

"Yeah," Anika replied with a nod. "He got me my own closet set up in his bedroom with all types of designer shit, Sadie! I almost fainted on the spot."

"Wow! So this is getting really serious now hun. You do know that?" Sadie questioned her with an arched brow. "This isn't just fucking anymore. This is a serious relationship between you and him."

"I know, I know, and I'm falling for him even more every single day Sadie. Most of my doubts about him have died down," Anika commented.

"Most?"

"Yeah... I still have one," she said quietly, looking down at her hands.

"And what's that?"

"Masika," Anika said with an eye roll. "I don't know what exactly went down with them. I'm not even one-hundred percent sure if they're over. He could be lying to me and I need to know for sure where she now stands in his life and where I now stand."

"I think he's done with Masika. If you say he's been with you all these past few weeks and it's getting serious, then he must be done with her. But still find out what you gotta find out girl. If it's going to be the thing that helps you decide your future with him, then so be it."

"Yeah, I gotta find out. When I do, I'll definitely know what I want with him for the future," Anika announced happily. "I know for a fact that I want to be with for a long time though."

***

"Baby, baby! What the fuck are you do-"

"Shut the fuck up!" Leek shouted loudly, cutting her off completely as he grabbed her by her hair and pulled her closer to him. "This is all your fucking fault!"

"Baby how?! I haven't done anythi- Leek, please let go of me! You're hurting me!" Masika exclaimed, now afraid of the way Leek was acting towards her. He had her by her hair and was now pulling her towards her bedroom. When they were finally inside, he flung her onto her double bed, making it bounce.

"Leek! What have I done?! Leek please, te- Leek, no! Leek, don't! Stop pointing the fuckin' gun at me! Leek please stop!"

"Shut the fuck up bitch," he barked angrily, still pointing his pistol at her. "If you never started fucking with that dude in the first place, you and I would be good. You wouldn't be fuckin' pesterin' me for some dumb divorce."

"Leek, we're not together anymore! Please!"

"I'm not divorcin' you Mas! You belong to me, not him. So dead that shit right here, right now if you wan' to keep yo' life," he threatened sternly, still pointing his black pistol at her as she lay terrified in the middle of her bed, looking up at him. He wasn't planning to shoot her, but if she didn't tell him what he wanted to hear, then he was going to.

"Okay," she answered quietly. "No divorce."

"You swear?"

Masika nodded, trying to reassure Leek that she was telling the truth. She wasn't. But she couldn't let him know that. She would have to figure out some way to get her divorce from him. There was only one man that she wanted to be married to, and it wasn't him.

"And you better tell that stupid nigga to stay off my back or else I'm going to put a bullet in his brain my damn self. He's already murked two of my best men and I won't hesitate to do the same to him. A'ight?"

Masika reluctantly nodded again, but when Leek's silver pistol was back up directly facing her she quickly spoke up. "I will! I promise!"

"Good," Leek stated with an evil grin. "Now get fuckin' naked. It's been a minute since I fucked that pussy.

CHAPTER 18 ~ LIES TO KEEP YOU HAPPY

What Leek had done last night had Masika on edge. She didn't like the fact that he had come so easily into her apartment without her permission. Then he had the audacity to pull a gun out on her? The nigga had lost his damn mind.

Thank God he hadn't asked anything about Tarique. He seemed to have forgotten about his own child but Masika saw this as a blessing in disguise. He was still staying with her mother at the moment because Auntie Jo in Florida had left town for a bit, but in the next coming weeks she would be back, and Masika would be sending Tarique on his merry way out to Florida.

Masika couldn't wait to get back with Blaze because she needed her man's assurance, love and protection. Protection especially away from Leek's crazy ass. She couldn't wait to be back with him.

She missed all the time they spent together, especially the time they spent making love. She couldn't wait for things to get back to normal between them again. He was her thug and she was his trap queen. No one else had the rightful title but her.

"Blaze's aunt invited you to her barbeque?" Masika looked up and was made to stare into the curious brown eyes of her sister. Masika nodded simply before looking down at her pasta, using her fork to pick one up and take a bite.

The Brooks' sisters were at an Italian restaurant, just spending the day together since they both didn't have anything better to do. Masika would rather have been with her man but he wasn't down to see her right now, it seemed.

"When is it?" Desiree queried.

"In about two weeks," Masika responded with a blank face.

"Aren't you happy? This is your chance," Desiree reminded her.

"My chance to do what?"

"See Blaze."

Masika's mood instantly brightened up. How could she have forgotten?! Blaze Aunt had invited her to her barbeque. A barbeque that Blaze was definitely going to be at. Blaze must have not told her that they weren't together at the moment, meaning that Blaze was planning to get back with her!

"Oh my gosh!" Masika exclaimed with joy, releasing what she had failed to realize before. "This is my chance to talk to him and get back together. If his aunt invited me then she had no clue of our break because he probably hadn't told her. Which means... He wants to get back together!"

"You really think so?" Desiree questioned her with a lifted brow, trying to disguise her sudden discontent attitude.

"Yes! I'm sure. Absolutely positive. By the time that barbeque is over, I'll be back with my man. And you'll have a front row to the reunion Des, because you're coming with me to the barbeque. It's gonna be wonderful!"

Masika couldn't wait for Blaze's aunt's barbeque to come. She knew that they were going to get back together and things between them was going to go back to normal. She just knew it.

***

Marquise: "Nah, lover boy's too preoccupied waiting for his girl to come out with us right now Kareem."

Kareem: "I know... The boy's been feening for the pussy all week."

Blaze stared down at his bright screen and couldn't help but chuckle at the way his boys were trying to tease him about his current situation. So what he was whipped? Anika was everything to him now.

Blaze: "Chill... I've missed her."

Kareem: "We kno' you've missed her..."

Marquise: "And that pussy too!"

Blaze laughed lightly, shaking his head as he looked at his phone clock, trying to work out when Anika would be here.

Blaze: "Any word on Leek?"

Kareem: "Nah... Still searchin'."

Marquise: "Since when did that nigga become so good at runnin'?"

Blaze: "Don't worry, we gon' get his ass. He can run but he can't hide."

Kareem: "Bet."

Suddenly, Blaze's front doorbell rang loudly, drawing Blaze's attention away from his group chat to the new visitor outside his door, who he was sure had to be his baby.

Blaze: "I'm out. Bonnie's here."

Blaze then quickly locked off his iPhone screen and got up out his seat. Bonnie was the nickname that the boys had given Anika ever since the test she had did worked. She had come out of Blaze's car to check on him and make sure he was good, and for that Blaze knew she was truly his ride or die.

Walking to his golden front door and seeing a figure stand on the other side of the door reminded him on how he wanted to pick her up and bring her here. However, she insisted that he not bother and that she could drive here herself. One thing he loved but also sometimes hated about her was the control she had over him. It was amazing in the bedroom, but sometimes out of the bedroom it pissed Blaze off.

As soon as he swung his door open and Anika was made to look up into those grey eyes, she swore she was in heaven. Clad in a white wife beater, black sweats and black socks, Anika's craving for him all week began to rapidly fire up again. No words needed to be said for them to know how much they missed and wanted each other.

Blaze smirked and quickly grabbed her by her waist and pulled her closer to him, so he could brand his plump lips down to hers. The kiss was sweet. Sweet, soft and seductive. Their tongues began to battle in lust and passion, not willing to stop and only building the hunger and desire for each other.

Anika's arms found their way around Blaze's neck and instantaneously, she felt her legs lifting off the ground and wrapping around his torso. He began to lead her into his home, the door shutting behind her.

"Blaze... I've missed you... So much," Anika whispered passionately between their kisses.

"Missed... Yo' pretty ass... Too," he responded sweetly, pulling their lips apart with a soft snack and moving his lips to her neck. He could smell her sweet scent already and it was already sending his nerves running through the roof. The effect she had on him was one that he knew was never going to stop.

His seductive neck kisses had already began to drive her crazy and with each moan that left her mouth, she knew how bad she wanted her man right now. *We've only been away from each other for a week... Imagine a whole month?* Anika couldn't imagine it.

"Blaze... Baby, we need to talk though," Anika stated shyly, with a soft sigh.

"What... 'bout?" Blaze questioned her in between his seductive kisses up and down her neck. "We can talk later bae... Let me make you feel good first."

"Blaze... that feels really good but... stop for a sec."

"You... really want... me to?"

Anika nodded convincingly, making Blaze realize that what she wanted to talk about was serious.

Five minutes later, Blaze had been led to his living room by Anika, and was now sitting opposite her on his couch waiting for her to talk. Staring into those pretty brown eyes of hers and looking at that beautiful face of hers made him happy knowing that she was his. She belonged to him. No one else.

"Mali-"

He suddenly cut her off and lifted his hand to stroke her soft cheek. "You're so beautiful."

She blushed, glowing bright pink before lifting her hand to place on top of his. "Thank you."

"What'chu want to talk 'bout baby?" he queried, grabbing her hips and pulling her onto his lap.

"Well..." Anika turned to look at him before continuing, "I need to know if you're done with Masika for good."

Here we go with this bullshit again, Blaze mused annoyingly. He didn't want her to know that he hadn't actually talked to Masika since the last time she had popped up at his mansion. He didn't want her to think that he still wanted Masika. So he did the next best thing. He lied.

"Baby, I ended shit with her weeks ago. I ain't with her anymore. I'm with you because I want to be with you. You only."

What else could he say? He didn't want to lose her. Not now that he was falling deeply in love with her. He couldn't lose her. The best bet for him would be to lie and then sort Masika out before the end of the month.

"You the only chick I want. No one else. Who else am I gon' give this dick to? You only Anika."

Lies... Lies... Lies...

Blaze's thoughts instantly flashed back to last week, at Cheetah Lounge. What a nasty, freaky night that had turned out to be.

"What the fuck you doin' here Desiree?" Blaze asked her rudely, watching her as he sat on his office chair. She gave him a sexy grin before locking his office door and turning to face him.

"I said, what the fuck are you doin' here Desiree?"

She didn't bother responding though. Instead, she began walking closer to him and once walking around his mahogany table, she began to strip. She slowly began unbuttoning her brown trench coat, both eyes still on him.

"Desiree. Get the hell..." His words trailed off once she was completely naked in front of him. The brown trench coat was now on the floor and Desiree's sexy, naked body was now revealed to him. Blaze couldn't stop his dick from getting hard even if he tried.

And once she got down on her knees and started unzipping his jeans, pulling down his boxers and lifting his dick out, Blaze was no longer in control of how his dick was behaving.

That night was one of the most unexpected nights in Blaze's life. He hadn't expected Desiree to come see him that night and start giving him head. He hadn't expected her to start using her tits to rub against his dick. He hadn't expected her to spit all on him and suck him completely dry. And he certainly hadn't expected to fuck her.

So staring into Anika's eyes and telling her that she was the only one who had gotten this dick, was a lie. A lie that Blaze knew he shouldn't have had to lie about in the first place. Why the hell had he cheated on his dream girl? Why'd he have to act like such an idiot all of a sudden? Fuck temptations from a freaky bitch! If he loved Anika, why was he giving what belonged to her, to the next bitch? Why the hell was he back messing around with Desiree?

All this shit had to stop now. He couldn't lie or cheat on the girl he loved anymore, or else he knew he was going to lose her. And losing Anika would be the biggest regret of his life.

CHAPTER 19 ~ BLAZE'S BITCHES

"You look so sexy baby… I can't wait to get back home and strip you out that dress again," Blaze whispered sexily in her ear as they walked hand in hand towards his aunt's oak front door. All Anika could do was blush happily and move into her man, so she could plant a sweet kiss on his cheek.

When the door swung open, Anika and Blaze were greeted by Sadie who had one of Blaze's little cousins, Jayda, in her arms. Jayda was one of Aunt Ari's daughters and she was only eleven months, turning one next month. She was the cutest baby ever and as soon as she laid her eyes on Blaze, she began reaching out to him.

"Mali! Mali!" She called out to him innocently, making Anika smile at how happy and excited she was to see him.

"Hey lil' mama." Blaze quickly picked her up out of Sadie's arms, gave her a kiss on her forehead and walked into the house, playing with her. Seeing Malik act so lovingly and soft around his little cousin, brought joy to Anika's heart. It started making her ponder on how things would be if she had babies from him and how he would always be down to look after them. *Too early Anika… Way too early.*

"Girl, you look beautiful!" Sadie exclaimed brightly, making Anika spin around so she could examine her outfit.

Anika knew she looked good. She had worked over three hours trying to piece her outfit together for today. She needed to look good, not just for Blaze, but for his aunt, too. Clad in a long nude bodycon skirt, nude Louboutins and a matching lace bralet crop top, with gold jewelry on her wrists, neck, ears and even ankles, Anika knew she was looking like one bad bitch.

"Thank you Sadie! You look... good too," Anika stated sheepishly, looking up and down at her best friend in jeans, nude heels and a simple white tee.

"Bitch shut up, you know I'm not looking that good... Yet," she responded with a smirk. Anika guessed that she was going to change into something better later on.

Ten minutes later, Anika had greeted all of Sadie's relatives. Some she had met before at the last barbeque and some new ones that she was just meeting for the first time. It wasn't until she was playing blackjack with a few of Blaze's uncles that Blaze had popped up out of nowhere and was telling her that he needed her to come with him.

He led her near the cooking barbeque, where his auntie was. He quickly explained to Anika, privately, that he wanted to tell his aunt about them, but he wanted to do it with her by his side. Once near her, Anika greeted her warmly and received a warm reply and hug. Then Blaze got right to it.

"Auntie... Anika and I are together."

Anika was nervous all of a sudden and she didn't understand why. Sure, she had met Sadie's god mother before, but meeting her now as Blaze's girlfriend was scary. She wasn't sure how she was going to react towards her knowing that she was now with her nephew.

Looking from Blaze's handsome face to his aunt's, who stood opposite them both, with a bowl of potato salad in her petite hands, Anika found herself trying her hardest to remain calm. From the look in his aunt's eyes, she was very surprised. Angry? No. More shocked by the revelation from Blaze.

"You're what?" she queried Blaze, looking from Anika to her nephew.

"We together Auntie," Blaze repeated, grabbing hold of Anika's warm hand and gently squeezing it in his. "We in a relationship together."

"What about Masika?" she asked him with a serious look.

"Masika and I are over," Blaze stated sternly. "We broke up."

"Oh shit," his Aunt cursed with an open mouth. "Well congratulations to you two but... Malik... There's somethin' I need to tell you."

"What is it?"

"I'd rather talk to you in private Malik," she informed him firmly. "No offense Anika honey."

Blaze wanted his aunt to reveal what she had to say in front of him and Anika, but Anika reassured him that it was cool if he talked to her in private. Anika was sure that whatever she had to say, Blaze would report back to her anyway. No matter how good or bad it was, she was going to know about it.

So while Blaze and his aunt headed back inside the house to talk, Anika was left alone. Sadie had disappeared off somewhere to change her outfit, so Anika headed back to Blaze's uncles to finish off her card game with them.

However, as she looked on she saw a female now sitting in her seat. She couldn't see her face but she seemed to have taken her spot in the card game already.

"Anika, you come back to join the game?" Uncle Roy questioned her curiously.

The female turned her head and looked straight at Anika with a frown. Seeing who it was that had taken her spot in the game and seat, made Anika almost faint on the damn spot. But then she reminded herself that Blaze was no longer with her. He had broken up with her.

So who the hell had invited this bitch?

***

"You did what?!"

"Ay, don't go shouting at me boy! This isn't my fault," Ari responded simply. "If you had told me before then I wouldn't have invited her."

"Since when did you start invitin' her without tellin' me first Auntie?" Blaze queried angrily.

"I wasn't thinking about whether or not you guys were together. You're engaged, so I acted upon inviting her like I normally would. She was your fiancée a few months ago, right? I wasn't aware of your breakup until now Malik. You should have told me."

All Blaze could do was stay silent and try to remain calm. He was just praying that Masika didn't bother showing up tonight. They were over. He hadn't talked to her in months. She didn't need to show face. He was praying she didn't turn up.

Unfortunately, all Blaze's prayers were completely pointless now that he could hear shouting coming from the barbeque outside.

"Bitch, you the one that stole my man!"

Blaze groaned deeply with annoyance at the fact that he could hear Masika's voice right now and then he quickly rushed out.

Masika was currently being held back by Desiree and Uncle Roy, while Anika stood with her arms crossed and watched with a large smile at the fact that she couldn't get closer to her.

"I don't get why you're so angry... So much anger," Anika cooed gently, purposely doing it to fuck with Masika. "You need to relax."

Seeing Desiree here now, only added to his current frustrations and anger. She was here. Masika was here. And so was Anika. The three women in his life that he had some type of relation with.

"Bitch I'll fuck you u-"

Blaze suddenly cut her off, "You ain't gon' do shit, Masika."

She suddenly became quiet and turned to face him, her eyes softening because of his presence. "Baby… I've missed you."

Blaze rolled his eyes at her before answering, "Missed who? You kno' we over."

"No we're not," she snapped.

"Yes we are Masika. We not together anymore," he reminded her.

"I don't know what this bitch has done to you Blaze, but we're still together. I don't have a son with Leek. We're engaged to be married, you need to stop playin' these games boy. I miss and love you. I want to be with you again. And you want to be with me too, or else why was I invited by your aunt and why have you not ended things with me?"

Blaze badly wanted to snitch on Desiree and everything she had told him about Masika having a son with Leek. But he didn't want to create a bigger hole for Masika than there was already. And he certainly didn't want Desiree running her mouth about them fucking.

"Masika, we're over."

"So why do I still have the ring you gave me baby?" she asked softly. "You still have my apartment key and you've sti-"

"Yeah I still have your apartment key but all that don't mean shit Mas," he barked. "I'm wit' Anika now. And you just goin' to have to accept things and get over it. I'm not wit'chu anymore."

"But you're still fucking me Blaze!" she shouted loudly, trying to escape Uncle Roy's grip.

Huh? Blaze had no clue what she was currently talking about. As far as he was concerned, he hadn't touched Masika since two months ago. He never went over to her apartment. Just because he had a key didn't mean that he used it.

"You're what?" Anika finally spoke up. Her facial expression, angry and shocked. "You fucked her Malik?"

"No baby, I ain'-"

"Yeah, he's been fuc-"

"Shut yo' ass up!" Blaze fumed, making everyone at the barbeque who had been mumbling and muttering amongst themselves, shut up completely. That's how powerful his voice was right now. Masika's lying was bringing out a side of his that he didn't like to show around family. He could feel Anika drifting away from him and he wasn't liking it. "I ain't fuckin' her Nika, I'm fuckin' you," he stated, trying to convince Anika. He began sauntering closer to her so she could hold onto her, but she kept taking steps back away from him.

"Anika... Bae, please believe me, I ain't fuckin' her."

"But you been fuckin' me nigga!" Desiree suddenly protested, making Anika freeze still in her tracks. "You don't want neither of these bitches Blaze, 'cause you want me. You fucked me in my apartment a few weeks ago and last week, at Cheetah Lounge. So just end all this shit so we can be together."

Lord please tell me this a dream, Anika mused silently. *This must be a dream. Because there's no way these bitches are claiming that they've been fucked by my man.*

But when Anika noticed how Blaze had suddenly kept silent after the chick that had come with Masika, remarks, she knew it was true.

"You've... You've..." She couldn't even make out her words properly. All her emotions were running high and it seemed like all she wanted to do was burst into tears. But no way was she going to do it in front of all these people, watching her.

"Anika, I'm so-"

"Save it," she snapped, pushing him away from her and storming out Auntie Ari's garden and heading inside her home. She needed to go far, far, far away from here. There was no point of her staying here anymore.

The quicker she walked towards the exit, the more it seemed that Blaze was fast on her trail, following her and begging her to listen to him. "Anika! Please just hear me out!"

How could she stand around and listen to the man who had humiliated her? He had cheated on her with the next bitch and made her to believe that she was the one that he wanted. What a bunch of fucking lies!

As soon as she made it to the front door and began to open it, he quickly slammed it shut with his hand making her sigh, now frustrated that he wouldn't leave her the fuck alone. "Anika please! Stop!"

She didn't bother turn round to face him and that hurt him even more knowing that she couldn't bear to look at him. If someone had told him five hours before this barbeque that he would be losing his woman, he wouldn't have bothered to come in the first place.

"Baby, I never meant to hurt you," he whispered softly behind her. "I love you."

Hearing him say it for the first time was supposed to be a happy moment. But all she found herself doing was bursting into tears because of how heartbroken she was. It was all his fault. His fault because she loved him too.

"You slept with Masika and that other chick," she said through gritted teeth. "You never even ended things with Masika, you lied!"

"I didn't sleep with Masika and I'm sorry I lied about ending things with her," he responded sadly. But when he didn't say anything else, Anika knew that the other chick and him had definitely messed around and all she had said about them fucking in her apartment and at Cheetah Lounge was true. "Desiree was a mistake," he explained, placing his hand on the side of her waist. "A mistake I ain't gon' make again because I don't want her. I wan' you Anika. I love you."

As sweet as his words and touch felt, Anika knew it was too good to be true. Why was it always her that was falling for the grimy, stupid, cheating ass niggas? The niggas that didn't really care about her feelings and would rather be cuddled with the next bitch than her.

Anika shrugged his hand away and pushed him away from her. She still kept her back turned facing him though. She knew looking into his eyes would probably cause her to tell him how much she loved him too. "You don't love me Malik. You love Masika or Desiree, I don't know! I don't care. I'm not doing this anymore."

"Baby no, I want to be wit' yo-"

"Leave me alone Malik!" she shouted angrily at him, as she opened the door ready to get away from here. She stepped out into the cool air before turning to face him with teary, sad eyes. "We're over."

"No! Anika, don't yo-"

She slammed the door in his face.

CHAPTER 20 ~ UNEXPECTED APPEARANCES

"You see the fight Masika and Desiree had before I kicked their asses out? Hilarious," Auntie Ari commented with a chuckle, trying to brighten up the mood but seeing that it wasn't working. "Look Blaze, I know you didn't mean for all this shit to happen today, but this is all your fault boy."

"I kno' Auntie," he mumbled.

"You shouldn't have cheated on Anika and you should have ended things with Masika, if you were serious about Anika from the start," she advised him.

"I kno' Auntie," he repeated with a small sigh.

"How many times you called her?"

"Thirty."

"And she ain't picked up once, right?"

Blaze nodded sadly, before looking down at his blank phone screen. He just wanted to know if she was okay or not. He needed to know if she had made it home safely.

"You need to give her some space… That's all she really needs right now," Auntie Ari informed him gently. "And you need space to figure out what you really want."

"What'chu mean Auntie?" he queried.

"Don't act dumb with me boy," she told him, with a small suck of her teeth. "You need to decide what you're doing about Anika and Masika."

"I love Anika."

"But you also loved Masika," she reminded him. "You were engaged to her, still are. All the time you were with Anika, you never once went to see Masika and tell her that you were never getting back with her."

Blaze kept silent for a while, pondering in his own thoughts and thinking about what Aunt Ari had just told him. "Desiree told me she had a son with Leek, so I figured shit was over between us."

"But you never personally checked up on it yourself Malik," she said. "You were too busy with Anika to realize that you hadn't actually found out the real truth. And even if you had, you never once put Masika in her place and told her that you weren't with her anymore. Failing to do all this tells me... You still love that girl."

Blaze wasn't sure. He loved Anika, he knew that for sure, but Masika? Now that was a whole other situation all together. Being away from her for a month was refreshing he couldn't lie. But not once had he bothered to get in contact with her and set her straight. Instead, he blocked and avoided her.

"So what'chu think I should do Auntie?" he asked helplessly.

"I think you need to seek some closure with her before you move on and try to work things out with Anika. Find out if she really has a son with Leek and find out if you still love her, because there's no point in stringing Anika along if you're in love with another woman Malik."

***

"You found him?"

"Yeah we found him B'," Kareem responded happily. "I can text you the location and we'll meet Marq there."

Leek had been found. This was the only good thing to happen to Blaze tonight. He couldn't wait to get his hands on that nigga and squeeze the living day lights of him. He deserved that and much more. Much, much, much more.

"I gotta do somethin' real quick, but yeah, text me the details and I'll meet you guys there."

Blaze knew he had to do this. He needed to know the truth. He needed to know if Masika was still the woman he wanted to be with. As much as he loved Anika, bringing her into his lifestyle wasn't a very good idea from the start, and Blaze knew this but still, he ignored it. Now he couldn't ignore it though. The time for him to make a decision was now.

Blaze cut his engine off and quickly stepped out his Lambo. His door went flying up in the air and once out, he pushed it closed. He began to fumble in his back pocket for Masika's apartment keys and once finding them, he was in front of her door ready to enter.

As soon as he pushed the key through the lock, he was greeted to the loud sounds of the television playing and when making his way deeper inside the apartment, a young boy sat on Masika's beige loveseat.

"Who you?" he asked Blaze with curious eyes, staying still on his seat.

"I'm... Blaze," he responded calmly, not knowing what to really do or say. An introduction would do for now. "Who are you?"

"Tarique," he replied shyly.

Tarique. Blaze was sure that he had heard that name before. It took him a few seconds to remember that Desiree was the one that had told him about Tarique. Masika and *Leek's* son.

So this is him, Blaze mused. *Desiree was tellin' the truth. Masika was lyin' to me all this time and thought she could get away with it. That bitch.*

"Where's yo' mom?"

Tarique instantly pointed towards the corridor leading to Masika's bedroom.

"And why's the TV so damn loud?" Blaze queried before grabbing the nearby television remote and lowering the volume, only to wish he hadn't.

"Mom said," Tarique answered simply.

"Fuck me just like that... Yessss!" Loud female moans immediately sounded through the apartment and Blaze's anger quickly began to build. *This bitch has her son in here, while she's fuckin' some nigga?*

"Ooooo, you fuck me better than my nigga!" To make things worse, Blaze's anger only increased when he realized that the nigga in there was most likely her baby daddy, Leek, the man he was supposed to kill tonight. Blaze didn't bother gloating around anymore. He was going to kill two people tonight. Leek and Masika.

He was fast on his heels, towards her bedroom and when finally reaching the door, Blaze turned the brown door knob and burst into the room.

The whole room reeked of sex, pussy and dick. And looking ahead, Blaze instantly noticed Masika bent over with Leek behind her, fucking her from the back. They were both turned facing the headboard so they hadn't seen him come in yet. The sight made him pull out his pistol from his back and lift it towards them.

Suddenly all hell broke loose when Masika turned around and saw Blaze standing in her doorway, with his silver pistol pointed towards her. Her screams immediately filled the room and she pushed Leek away from her, making Blaze smirk at how petrified she was now.

"Blaze! No! Please put the gun down!"

This will teach her dumb ass to not lie to me ever again, Blaze mused happily. However, as soon as Masika began reaching for her covers to cover her naked body, Blaze suddenly noticed the dude lying next to her.

And he wasn't Leek.

His happy smirk instantly faded once he recognized the guilty face of his right-hand man. The man who was supposed to meet him in half an hour at Leek's current location. The man that he thought he could trust with his entire life and empire.

Mr. Marquise Lewis.

~ To Be Continued ~

DO NOT FORGET TO LEAVE A REVIEW!
~ A Note From Miss Jen ~

Thank you so much for reading Miss Jenesequa's novel.

Please do not forget to drop a review on Amazon, it will be greatly appreciated and I would love to hear what you thought about this novel! Don't forget to check out her other works:

- *Lustful Desires: Secrets, Sex & Lies*
- *Sex Ain't Better Than Love 1*
- *Sex Ain't Better Than Love 2*
- *Luvin' Your Man: Tales Of A Side Chick*
- *Down For My Baller 1*
- *Down For My Baller 2*
- *Bad For My Thug 1*

Feel free to connect with Miss Jenesequa at:

Twitter: @MissJenesequa - https://www.twitter.com/MissJenesequa

Instagram: @Missjenesequa_ - http://www.instagram.com/missjenesequa_/

Facebook Page: Miss Jenesequa –

- https://www.facebook.com/AuthorMissJenesequa

And join her readers group for exclusive sneak peaks of upcoming books and giveaways!

- *https://www.facebook.com/groups/missjensreaders/*

E-mail:
msjenesequa@gmail.com
Website: www.missjenesequa.com

Please make sure to leave a review! I love reading them. Thank you so much for the support and love. I really do appreciate it!

Miss Jenesequa

Text ROYALTY to 42828 to keep up
with our new releases!

Looking for a publishing home?

Royalty Publishing House, Where the Royals reside, is accepting submissions for writers in the urban fiction genre. If you're interested, submit the first 3-4 chapters with your synopsis to submissions@royaltypublishinghouse.com. Check out our website for more information: www.royaltypublishinghouse.com.

Be sure to <u>LIKE</u> our Royalty Publishing House page on Facebook

CPSIA information can be obtained
at www.ICGtesting.com
Printed in the USA
LVHW021535060519
616793LV00001B/203/P